D1359482

DRASTIC
PARK

Also by W. E. Davis
in Large Print:

Suspended Animation
Victim of Circumstance
Black Dragon

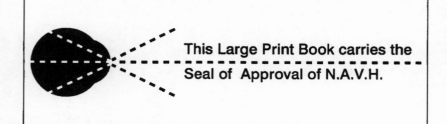

This Large Print Book carries the
Seal of Approval of N.A.V.H.

DRASTIC PARK

A GIL BECKMAN MYSTERY

W. E. Davis

Thorndike Press • Thorndike, Maine

Published in 1998 by arrangement with Crossway Books, a division of Good News Publishers.

Thorndike Large Print ® Christian Fiction Series.

The tree indicium is a trademark of Thorndike Press.

The text of this Large Print edition is unabridged. Other aspects of the book may vary from the original edition.

Set in 16 pt. Plantin by Al Chase.

Printed in the United States on permanent paper.

Library of Congress Cataloging in Publication Data

Davis, Wally, 1951–
    Drastic Park : a Gil Beckman mystery / W.E. Davis.
     p.   cm.
    ISBN 0-7862-1403-1 (lg. print : hc : alk. paper)
    1. Large type books.   I. Title.
    [PS3554.A93785D73   1998]
    813'. 54—dc21   98-9954

To
Dean Gunter

ONE

The light from flickering torches danced off the irregular stones in the cobbled street as a slight chill, a harbinger of an even colder night to come, hung over the square. A stone cherub at the top of a circular fountain in the center of the square endlessly poured from a pot, the water gurgling pleasantly as it spilled into three levels of shallow bowls, ever increasing in size from top to bottom.

Shops were open, their window displays inciting covetousness in passing peasants. The large hats and gaily colored tunics of the shopkeepers, worn over puffy-sleeved shirts, cried out for attention.

People of all ages, most of them commoners, meandered through the square, admiring the thatched roofs and the quaint gingerbread decorations on the shops. Intricately carved wooden signs adorned with French-sounding names announced to those who could read what awaited inside. Hawkers beckoned the passersby to come in. Some heeded, some did not, but all the merchants were good-natured regardless. The sweet plunks and strums of a wandering minstrel's lyre wafted over the square, providing a soothing background to the footfalls and murmurings of the crowd.

Suddenly the strumming ceased, and a loud cry at one end of the street drew the attention of all. The peasants all stopped what they were doing, turning their heads in the direction of the agitated voice to see what was amiss.

Into the square strode a handsome man with long black hair cascading from under his dark feather-plumed hat to lightly dust his shoulders. His nose cast a shadow over a thin delicate mustache, below which his mouth drew up in a sneer. His neck was surrounded by a white lace-edged collar. His long red velvet shirt was girded about the waist with a wide leather belt, another crossing his torso from right shoulder to the opposite hip, upon which rode the hilt of a menacing sword, sheathed in a leather scabbard.

The musketeer's shiny black boots clicked impertinently upon the cobblestones as he pointed a gloved finger at a man similarly dressed, stepping now into view at the opposite end of the square. Seeing this second armed man, the peasants obligingly scurried toward the fringes of the square, some of them dragging puzzled urchins behind them, leaving the cobblestones between

8

the two men empty.

"You, sir," shouted the red-tunicked swordsman, "have offended me the last time." He stopped, not quite in the center of the square, and waited for an answer. All eyes turned expectantly toward the anticipated responder, whose costume was of green silk and signified, by its garishness alone, that its wearer was of a higher station in society than his accuser.

"Do you address me, knave?" he asked with a haughty air.

"He is a clever man indeed," mocked the first. "He knows it is to him I speak."

The aristocrat glanced around at the spectators and rolled his eyes, then addressed the man in red.

"If you feel you have a debt to collect, then state it. Have I stolen your purse? No, I think not. Air is free, and that is what your purse no doubt contains." He put his finger to his chin and looked up, deep in thought. "Ah, your maiden. That would be a possibility to be sure, but too easy a challenge. I wouldn't bother."

"Don't toy with me, sir. It is my honor with which you have trifled," announced the man in red, perturbed at his opponent's haughty attitude.

The man in green silk strode forward and

9

squinted theatrically at his accuser. "Have we met?"

The crowd chuckled, and he glanced about with a smirk, acknowledging their appreciation.

"Nay, sir, we have not, but I have received word from a most reliable source — your chambermaid, to be precise — that you have besmirched my family name."

The man in green dropped his head, sighed, and regarded his opponent. "If you mean to kill me, as I suspect to be the reason for the odious challenge you are obviously leading up to — at great length, I might add — will you please get on with it? I have business to attend to. What is your family name, and how have I damaged the goodness of it?"

"Very well, I'll play your game," the man in red rejoined. "My name is D'Artagnon. You recently spoke of my father, God rest his soul, as a coward, though he gave his life valiantly in the king's service."

"Ah." Green Silk nodded his head. "That was I," he said gaily.

"And you shall pay for that indiscretion with your life."

Green Silk yawned.

"Bye the bye," the accuser continued, "how many names have you dishonored recently so that you are unsure of which name I spoke?"

"Twelve," declared the aristocrat, quickly counting on his fingers, "not including the one I am preparing to disparage this afternoon." He looked at the crowd and smiled. "I have an appointment for lunch," he added to some bystanders.

"It is a wonder you are still alive," proclaimed the man in red. "Are there no men your better, or do they swallow your insults and scurry away with their tails tucked between their legs?"

"Some of one, some of the other," he answered, tugging on his gloves. "But most fall to this." And with a ringing flourish he pulled his sword from its scabbard in a quick, easy motion. "Now, knave, *en garde.*"

"With pleasure!" The man in red drew his weapon also, and the two bounded toward each other, sabers flashing and clanging as they fought. Each thrust was answered with a parry, each slash with a feint, each swing with a duck or a jump as they stepped lively around the square, around the fountain, over the fountain, even through the fountain, with neither party able to gain the advantage and thrust steel home.

Then a metallic clatter filled the air, prompting a gasp from the crowd as if from

11

a single person, as a sword fell to the ground.

The aristocrat in green silk stood with his feet spread wide, the tip of his sword at the throat of his combatant as the knave sat on the pavement with his back against the fountain bricks. The crowd pressed in for the kill, but just before the sword was driven home, a woman cried out from a nearby second-floor balcony, "No, sire! I beg you, spare him!"

The aristocrat, his elbow raised for leverage, hesitated as he ventured a glance up toward the woman who stood with her arms out, pleading. Her peasant dress and apron could not hide her full figure, and her head was covered by a large cap, her hair tucked underneath. A domestic woman.

D'Artagnon squirmed, but his conqueror did not relent.

"Uh, uh," the victor cautioned, wagging a finger, and D'Artagnon ceased his fidgeting. The aristocrat looked back up at the window. "And why, good madam, should I do so?"

"He is but a foolish man," she said. D'Artagnon stuck his tongue out at her but pulled it in quickly and smiled sheepishly when his opponent glanced down at him. "His father is alive and runs a bakery in Paris. My husband fancies himself a musketeer, but he failed the entrance exam."

The crowd laughed, and she continued, "Please, kind sir, let him go and I'll . . ." She paused and looked at her prone husband, whose panic-stricken face begged for silence. She waved him off. "I will roast you some mutton this evening. You can stop by for dinner on your way home from killing a more worthy adversary. We would be pleased to have you. Wouldn't we, Pierre?"

Pierre — the former D'Artagnon — nodded emphatically and with a thumb and an index finger carefully removed his opponent's sword from the nape of his neck.

Green Silk sheathed the blade and helped his opponent up. "See you for supper then?"

"Glad to have you," Pierre said. They shook hands and turned with a flourish, striding their separate ways to a rousing round of applause from the peasants.

I was impressed. This was a new feature here at the theme park — to supplement the gunfights in the Western Town and the gangsters versus the cops rat-a-tat-tats in the Flapper Zone — and it was a good one. There were several scenarios, but the stunt men were very capable with their swords and responded to visual signals from each other, changing their performance each time.

Their script wasn't set in concrete, and

D'Artagnon changed his name frequently to try and crack the other players up. He had been de Gaulle, Pepe Le Peu, and Clousseau already this week. This prevented boredom in the actors, in addition to livening up the show for the guests.

The weapons were dull, with no points, but the stunt men still wore ballistic vests, the kind the cops wear, just in case. That was my idea. But I was no longer involved in any of that. I was back in security now, working graveyard. Had been for a week. I didn't mind so much. At least I could enjoy the park without all the visitors to distract me. And I still looked snappy in the uniform.

As I coursed somewhat aimlessly through the dispersing crowd, I caught the eye of Green Silk just before he disappeared through an employee gate and gave him a salute. He returned it with a tip of his hat and disappeared. Green Silk was a friend of mine, a guy who used to work in security but had finally been able to join the ranks of the stunt men, which is what he'd wanted to do in the first place. I had even sparred with him a couple of times with fencing foils just to keep him in tune for his stint in the stunt show, something I'd learned in my college days.

My attention once again focused ahead of

me, I saw someone familiar and pulled up short. I hoped he wouldn't see me, but it was too late. He caught my eye, and a wicked smile broke slowly onto his face. With his wife and daughter in tow he headed directly toward me, and I was trapped. I waited, thinking of all the things I could say to him, knowing I would say none of them.

"Gilbert!" he greeted in that syrupy way of his that reeked of insincerity. "Long time no see. How have you been?"

I smiled, somewhat passively. "Bill. I've been fine. And yourself?"

Captain William "Don't Call Me Bill" Fitzgerald winced at his hated nickname, but I continued, ignoring his pain and not waiting for an answer to my question since I really didn't care. "Got Harry Clark to comp you in, I see. Good deal. Beats paying what they charge these days."

Captain Fitzgerald hated gratuities. Any cop caught accepting free coffee or a meal discount was disciplined, usually three days off without pay for a first or second offense, firing for the third regardless of how trivial. I'm not saying his policy was necessarily bad; it was just that he applied it to everyone but himself. He put on a big show in public, getting into shouting matches with the local donut shop folks over a cup of coffee they wouldn't accept his money for, but every Christmas he would receive bottles of hooch from local merchants and businessmen. He even got a new car at actual dealer cost from a local dealership, the owner of which just happened to be in the same community service organization as Fitzgerald.

He didn't dignify my comment with a response. He didn't have to. His face told me I was right about Harry Clark, the security manager, getting him in free. He quickly changed the subject.

"So, how do you like being a security guard, Gilbert, ol' boy? Not quite the same as being a cop, eh?"

"Different color uniform," I said, "and no gun. That's about it." I noticed the distinct absence of a thank you from him for solving two murders and several other serious crimes for him recently. Not that I was surprised.

"And much lower pay," he reminded me, "not to mention your status in the public's eye." He grinned wryly, thinking he was getting on my nerves. I yawned.

"Say," he said suddenly, "I notice you're not in uniform. You just hanging out, nowhere to go? Must be tough, not having any friends or a wif— ow!" Fitzgerald's wife stuck him in the ribs with an elbow. She knew about Rebecca and her unexpected

16

death a few years back. At least *she* had some sense of decorum.

Fitzgerald cleared his throat, as if by doing so he could regain control of the conversation, and said, "Well, there's more fun to be had. We'll be seeing ya, Gilbert."

I watched him as he walked off with his family, wondering how his wife had stood him all these years and feeling sorry for his daughter. She looked to be in extreme pain to be with him. I didn't watch him long, though — life is too short to waste it. I turned away and headed in the opposite direction.

My shift didn't start for another couple of hours, but I had come in early to wander around in my civvies to see how everything was going. The place was shaping up nicely now that most of the construction had been completed. The Dragon was running flawlessly. Moon Raiders had garnered a great deal of praise and national recognition. Everett the Dinosaur was a hit with all ages — not just the character costume version, but the comic strip too. He was already in twenty-five newspapers across the country, and there was talk of an animated movie and a Saturday morning cartoon show.

Just talk, mind you, but you never know what could happen.

Speaking of Joey Duncan — and I was, because he drew the strip and any other art work they needed of the little dinosaur — I wondered if he would be ready in the morning when I got off duty. We were finally leaving for a week at the lake with Harold Curran — a week of fishing and rock climbing — Joey watching me fish and me watching Joey climb rocks. It was a vacation I had been wanting and needing for quite some time now.

That I had been able to work at all this week was pretty good, I thought. I was still a little shaken and sore from my latest escapade — a fight with a scrappy Japanese kid and a death dangle off the roller coaster. But I figured all I had to do was walk around, lock and unlock doors, shine my flashlight at things, and hope I didn't find any dead bodies. I could do all that in a wheelchair.

Besides, in spite of everything I'd said about the park in times past, I really enjoyed working here, even in security. It was like a paid vacation in a sense — getting to walk around the place at night, poking around where the public wasn't allowed, seeing how things worked, strolling through the bewitching ambience of the Western Town, the quaint, narrow cobbled streets of the European Village, the chrome and white marble avenues of the Future Zone, the Depression-era metropolis of the Flapper Zone.

Yep, like a paid vacation. A low-paid vacation.

Everything reminded me of my upcoming vacation. It had been years since I'd drowned some worms and breathed crystal mountain air while sipping coffee in the bow of a fishing dingy, with nothing to bother me except —

"Gil! How's it going?"

The shout behind me broke into my thoughts, and the image of fishing heaven dissolved as I turned to see who the culprit was.

D'Artagnon flashed a grin and a wave.

"Hey, what's up, Steve?" I asked.

"Saw you in the crowd," he said, catching up to me. "What did you think?"

"You thrust when you should have parried."

"That was part of the plan," he explained with a wave. "Next time I get to win." He was still in costume and bowed to a couple of grade school kids and their parents who were walking by, removing his hat and sweeping it low in front of him. When he recovered, we continued our stroll.

"So did it look realistic?" he continued.

"Yeah, great. How's the vest work?"

"It's hot. I don't know how cops can stand it."

"Consider the alternative."

All expression vanished from his face. "Oh, yeah. Anyway, I hear this sword fighting gig was your idea. Suits me fine. It's a nice break from the gunfight, a lot more tension. The crowd really gets into it."

"Yeah," I admitted, "I suggested it first. But other people put it together."

"Someone told me you put on a demonstration."

I grinned. "Yeah, a buddy of mine from church has a sword collection. He came with me, and we did a little demo. Not much though. Neither of us is any good. I took fencing in college so I wouldn't have to exert myself on the weight machine or by running around the track."

D'Artagnon smiled. "Don't blame you. Well, here's where I get off. See you later, Gil."

"Later, Steve — I mean, D'Artagnon."

The musketeer disappeared into the stunt persons' lounge and change room to get ready for his next event, and I continued my stroll through the park. This was quite a place, really. Despite the occasional goofy decision from management or the owners, this really was a good place to work, especially for the youngsters and the old-timers. Good bennies, flexible hours, profit sharing, decent wage in some categories, interesting work. It was just square pegs like me that didn't quite fit in.

It took me a while, but I have to admit, I'd learned to enjoy it here. And now I was settling back into security where I could hide at night, keep my nose clean, live frugally, and occasionally enjoy Sally Foster's company.

I checked my watch. The park would close in a half hour. An hour after that I'd be on duty. Having not yet had dinner, I decided to head over to the Future Zone for a grilled-green-cheese-from-the-moon burger and a large order of space fries, served in a cardboard space shuttle with its bay doors open.

I was within sight of the place when I noticed a large commotion. Someone was on the ground. A few people were kneeling beside him. The rest had gathered around to watch. A woman shouted something about paramedics, and an employee ran off.

Probably choking on a slice of the moon, I surmised. I sighed, ran the Heimlich maneuver through my mind, and trotted over to the fallen guest.

But he wasn't choking. He was on his back, his head toward me, and he wasn't

21

moving. Even at that odd angle I recognized that balding head, tiny shoulders, and distended stomach. The expression on his wife's face, crouching next to him, told me all I needed to know. William "Don't Call Me Bill" Fitzgerald was having a heart attack.

I shoved my way through the gawkers and knelt down beside him, giving Mrs. Fitzgerald an assuring look. Her worried face didn't share my confidence. Rather, a flicker of regret for the way her husband had recently spoken to me was apparent. I looked at her long enough to let her know I understood, then went to work.

"How long?" I asked no one in particular.

"A minute," someone answered. "Maybe two."

Establishing his airway, I put my ear to his mouth while looking at his chest but felt nothing and saw no movement. I pinched his nose — his bulbous, red, capillary-tracked alcoholic's nose — opened his mouth by pushing my thumb down on his chin, and prepared to give him four quick breaths.

I hesitated for a split second, fighting a sudden revulsion in the pit of my stomach, but saw again the fear in Mrs. Fitzgerald's eyes. With a silent prayer for the Lord's help,

I closed my eyes and bent to the task, then opened my left eye slightly, watching his chest rise and fall with each breath I gave him.

The taste and smell of stale alcohol permeated my senses, but I dismissed it as I checked his pulse. Nothing. I found his xiphoid process, that little sharp point at the base of his sternum, put the heel of my hand two fingers up, and began compressions.

Thirteen, fourteen, fifteen . . . back to his head and two more respirations, then once again to his chest. I heard someone call my name. Looking up without stopping my efforts, I spied Barry, one of the on-duty security officers, racing toward me, a clear plastic disposable CPR mouth guard in his hand. I acknowledged him, nodding toward Fitzgerald's head while maintaining compressions. He squatted down and positioned the mouth guard, then pronounced himself ready.

"Pulse," I said and stopped briefly to allow him to feel lightly on the side of Fitzgerald's throat.

"Negative," the security officer answered and gave Fitzgerald another breath.

We continued two-man CPR, but in a few minutes we were both beginning to tire. Normally we'd change positions, but I didn't know if he had another mouth guard. I asked, and he shook his head.

"You okay there?" I inquired.

Barry gave the victim a breath, then said, "Yeah, I'm fine," and I resumed compressions.

Another minute or two passed — it seemed longer, but I'm sure it wasn't — and we heard sirens in the distance, paramedics who brought with them fresh arms and lungs.

Russ Lefferts and a paramedic I didn't know soon trotted up as the crowd parted for them, like a miniature Red Sea. They carried the gear they'd set up and in short order were ready for us to stand clear. I gave my final compressions and Barry his final breath, and we scooted away, struggling to our feet but not leaving, curious as to the effect of our efforts.

Russ quickly attached the EKG machine and flipped it on. I was surprised at what I saw on the screen.

Fitzgerald had a pulse.

"Systole," Russell confirmed. "Weak but steady."

"Liter of Ringers," said his partner, who had been on the phone to the base hospital, relaying information. "And Dextran."

"Keep the Ambu bag going. Get the oxygen ready."

"Blood pressure 110 over 50, pulse 65."

A murmur ran through the crowd as the paramedics stabilized their patient, started an IV, and lifted him onto the newly arrived gurney. Mrs. Fitzgerald's face, although still strained, was perceptively less so as she followed her husband to the waiting ambulance.

Barry and I backed away, tired and relieved, and watched in silence as Fitzgerald was carted off. An employee from the Space Station grill brought us each a soda, which we guzzled in earnest. I confess to having mixed emotions at that moment. Satisfaction from a professional standpoint that we'd been able to revive Fitzgerald, disappointment it hadn't been someone I actually wanted to live.

Lest you judge me too hastily, understand what I had put up with from this man over the years: poor performance evaluations — unjustifiable on all points — when he was my patrol sergeant; denial of vacation requests, which he then took in my stead; cruel jokes about my wife's death behind my back; and since I had been employed at the park, not even under his control, he had tried many times to intimidate me into not investigating the murders and other crimes we'd had there — to no avail, naturally.

Even so, as Barry and I congratulated each other while listening to the ambulance drive off from the out-of-sight receiving gate, I silently prayed that God would preserve Fitzgerald and heal whatever had caused his heart attack.

I furrowed my brow and shook my head. Where did this compassion for my enemies come from? Was I still me? I quickly checked my reflection in a nearby window. There was that familiar face, perhaps somewhat worse for the wear but otherwise unchanged.

I shrugged, unable to account for my attitude, and headed toward the security office to get ready for work.

Oh, the unsearchable mysteries of God's grace.

TWO

Remarkably enough, other than Fitzgerald's heart attack, the night passed quietly with no unusual occurrences. On the eve of my vacation I had expected something to happen, something that would force a delay in my departure, if not force me to abandon it altogether.

But there were no intruders, no trespassers from the high school streaking across the park on a dare, no drunk drivers ramming their automobiles into our perimeter wall, no medical emergencies — carpenters sawing off their thumbs or painters overcome by toxic fumes — and no overnight thefts discovered by early-arriving management-types.

Most importantly, no dead bodies were located, despite my best efforts to find them. Not that I wanted there to be any, mind you, but I didn't want to clock out and have one turn up. That might prove embarrassing.

It's like walking the strip malls when I was back in uniformed patrol. If there was a smashed window and you weren't there to prevent it or catch the burglar, you'd better at least find it before the store owner showed up in the morning. There was very little worse to get called on the carpet for than working your beat all night and not finding the broken plate glass window with the empty display where televisions used to be.

Night turned to dawn without a mishap, however, and I took a second to sit down with a stretch and a yawn on the top of Solomon's Mountain. A staircase and a small door gave access to it, and my perch afforded a rather remarkable view of the park.

It was good to see how the park had expanded in the last year or so. The new rides and attractions, the upgrades and new façades to the old ones, the new landscaping everywhere, thanks to Mr. George Ozawa. He was still here, but I suspected he might soon be offered an important position by Mr. Kumi Hiromoto, owner of Hiro Industries of Japan, when the Japanese version of this theme park got off the ground. Although Ozawa spoke little Japanese, I thought he just might take his ancient father up on it. Ozawa was, after all, the rightful heir to Hiromoto's fortune, even though he didn't want it. In fact, he hadn't known Hiromoto was his father until a few weeks earlier.

I studied the Dragon, the black, twisting roller coaster, silhouetted against a sky beginning to blossom in early-morning pinks and oranges, and thought about Eric Hiromoto, the old man's grandson and black sheep of the family. They were very hush-hush about what had happened to him since they discovered his treachery, and Michelle Yokoyama — senior vice president of the park and a close friend of Ozawa — wouldn't say. Part of me believed she didn't know for sure, but I figured she still had a pretty good idea or at least suspected what the old man had done to him.

As I surveyed the tranquil scene below me, noting some of the things I'd had a hand in, such as Moonraiders and the new Time Machine, my thoughts turned to what I'd accomplished during the last year and a half. Not just the rides and attractions, but the murders I had solved, the thefts, the sabotage . . . A root of bitterness crept out of my subconscious mind and down into my heart.

I, Gil Beckman, had saved the park from certain ruin on several occasions. I'd saved hundreds of thousands of dollars in lost revenue and outright theft and potentially millions of dollars in lost royalties from the Japanese if Hiromoto had been injured or killed. Two murderers had been captured, another murder thwarted, innumerable injustices prevented — and I was rewarded by being put back into security and stuck on graveyard, a position a kid fresh out of high school could get. Meanwhile Jerry Opperman, the president of the park, who had single-handedly driven it to the brink of destruction, still sat in his motorized office chair twiddling his thumbs and collecting an obscenely large paycheck.

As bad as the Japanese Relocation Centers and slavery were, what was happening to me was *real injustice!*

You're being selfish.

I turned and looked over my right shoulder. The voice was as clear as if someone had been standing next to me, but no one was there.

You did a good job. You deserve recognition.

That came from my opposite side, and again no one was there. I pictured an angel whispering in one ear, and his twin, in a red suit with a forked tail, whispering in the other. Or perhaps I was so tired after being up all night, my thoughts had taken on a life of their own.

I thought about what I'd heard, and after asking God to forgive me for my self-indulgent attitude, I brushed the imaginary demon from my left shoulder and stood up. I wasn't about to let a year of learning to be content evaporate in a puff of smoke in a couple of seconds.

Whatever I had, God had given to me, and I should be happy about it. What I "deserved" was irrelevant. I deserved to die, and even worse. That I was still able to sit up here and watch the sun rise, that I could pick up a paycheck every two weeks, that I could even breathe was entirely reliant on the mercy and grace of the Lord.

My radio crackled. "Sam One, are you there?"

I pulled the radio from the leather case on my belt and keyed the mike. "Sam One," I said, trying not to sound too tired.

"Sam" was a sergeant's designation, but I had been put in charge this week since the regular supervisor was on vacation, someplace I'd also be in less than an hour.

"Sam One, respond to Wild Bill's Western Jewelry. The custodian's ready to exit. And when you get off duty, Mrs. Potter wants to see you."

Mrs. Potter? Lizzie Borden Potter? The Dragon Lady? What did she want? And what was she doing here so early? *Must be important,* I thought, but I selfishly hoped she didn't keep me too long. I could hear trout calling my name.

Gil. Get it?

"10-4," I answered. I put the radio back and squinted across the top of Solomon's Mountain so I could see the front of the jewelry store. Its window faced the square, and I could see the janitor inside, next to the display case. Strange . . . It was hard to tell at this distance, from this height, but he didn't look ready. He was still puttering around. Oh, well, maybe he called before he actually needed me, knowing it could be five or ten minutes before I got there.

I started to turn toward the hidden door (a regular door in the top of the mountain might look strange, so it was disguised as a crack in the rock) when something caused me to look back at the janitor one more time. He was bent over, fussing with the bag of his upright vacuum. It's not unusual for a sanitation engineer to be fussing with his vacuum bag, but he seemed to be putting something inside it. At least, there didn't seem to be anything in his hand when he pulled it out. He repeated his actions a couple of times, glanced around as if checking to see if he was being watched, then wheeled the vacuum to the door. The lights blinked out.

Retreating back into the mountain, I hurried down a couple of flights of stairs and onto the track, then hustled along it to the loading dock and jumped off, sliding down a rock slope and dropping the final five feet onto the midway. I withdrew my radio and called dispatch, asking them to have the custodial supervisor meet me at Wild Bill's.

I unlatched the door, and the custodian smiled at me, nodded a thank you, and wheeled out his vacuum and the rest of his cleaning supplies. Just then his supervisor, Dan Harris, arrived in his electric cart. After asking the janitor to wait there a second, I took Harris aside and told him what I'd seen.

"Look, I might be wrong," I said, positioning myself so I could watch the custodian while speaking to his boss. "I'm not accusing him of anything, but it looked mighty suspicious."

"We have to be careful," Harris said. "The last guy we accused of stealing sued us."

"He wasn't guilty?"

"Oh, he was guilty all right. We knew it, but we couldn't prove it. He must have known we were on to him and dumped the stuff before we got there."

"So why'd he sue?"

"We fired him anyway. Gave him a severance check, a good recommendation in writing, the whole bit."

"So what was his beef? Getting fired?"

Harris rolled his eyes. "Stress. The embarrassment made him ill. He got some quack doctor to support it. The park paid him off. In return he promised to keep quiet. You know how the park hates bad press."

Boy, did I know the park. All the management folk — especially Opperman — made most of their decisions based, not on good business sense, but on how it would read in the papers. Even decisions that no one outside the park would care about.

Say, maybe that was how Opperman kept his job. He knew something that could ruin the park if it got out — something like the owners were all cannibals or satanists. That's it, they were all Satan worshipers. Or voodoo practitioners. Yeah, that made sense. That would explain a lot of their decisions.

Then again, I knew enough to sink a few ships, and management wasn't afraid of me. Of course, I wouldn't do anything with what I knew, but still . . .

"Sometimes it just doesn't pay to be an upstanding moral individual," I lamented out loud.

"Huh?" the janitorial supervisor said.

"What?" I snapped out of another lack-of-sleep-induced mental break. "Oh, nothing. I was just thinking . . . we need to get a look at that bag. After all, it's the park's vacuum, isn't it?"

"Actually, no."

"Huh? What are you talking about? They bring their own vacuums to work?"

"He's an employee for a company we contract with," Harris explained. "I supervise, and the park pays his employer, who pays his wages and benefits. Technically he works *at* the park, but he works *for* the other company. They bring all their own equipment. It's part of the contract. That way we don't pay for supplies or maintenance on the machines."

"I'd forgotten about that. Anyway, we can't just sit here and let him walk out," I protested.

"If you're sure he stole something —"

"That's just it, I'm not. I saw him put something in that bag, but I don't know what." I stopped to think about it for a second, then said, "Why don't we try the direct approach? We'll ask him if we can look. If he says no — and he won't unless there's something in there besides dirt — we can be reasonably certain he's hiding something. And then we'll look anyway. If he says yes, we're in the clear."

"And if there's nothing in there?" the supervisor asked.

"If there's nothing in there, I'll tell him you made a terrible mistake and I'll see to it you're properly punished." His eyes popped, and his mouth opened to protest, but I held up my hand. "Just kidding. I'll explain what I saw, and he'll understand why I wanted to look. Don't worry, it'll be okay."

Harris shrugged. "Okay, but you're taking responsibility for this."

I shrugged. So what else was new?

I turned to the custodian. "Good morning," I said, walking back to him. His face showed concern, whether because he was guilty or because he was mystified, I couldn't tell. "Sorry to keep you waiting. Do you speak English?"

It was a valid question. Many of the custodial workers didn't.

"Yes," he replied, somewhat perturbed.

"Sorry. I had to make sure. I'm Gil Beckman with security."

"Yes, I've seen you this week. Are you new?"

Wait a minute, I thought, *I'm the interrogator here.*

"No. Recently transferred. I noticed, from a distance, that you were messing around in your vacuum bag inside the jewelry store. Mind if I take a look?"

"The jewelry store? No, go ahead."

"I mean your vacuum."

"You want to look in my vacuum? Why?"

"We've had some thefts recently," I ex-

36

plained. That much was true. I left out how they occurred and what was stolen. For all I knew, he'd been sneaking stuff out in his vacuum every night.

He fidgeted. Nervous guilt.

"And you believe I have stolen things and put them in my vacuum?"

"Not necessarily. I mean, it's possible. I'm just asking you to let me look. If you have nothing to hide, why would it matter?" The old "put him on the defensive" routine. Now he had to give consent or look guilty.

"I have nothing to hide," he said, and I took a step toward the appliance. He pulled it away from me. "But I have rights. I don't like being called a thief."

"He didn't call you a thief," Harris defended, probably thinking of the lawsuit I'd just instigated.

"Might as well have. He insinuated it."

"This is nuts," I said. "I'm sick and tired of everyone throwing their rights in my face and expecting me to cower." I moved forward quickly and snatched the vacuum out of his hand. "Gimme that. It's high time we stop letting every Tom, Dick, and . . . what's your name?" I glanced at his name tag. "Every Tom, Dick, and Pablo run this business for us." I unzipped the outer bag and reached inside, feeling around in the bottom.

There was nothing there.

"You only do this because I am Hispanic," Pablo said.

I ignored him and fished around some more, thinking maybe he shoved the items under something. Nothing, though I did notice something that attracted my attention.

"See?" Pablo asserted. "I told you. You're in big trouble now."

I looked up at him, daring him with my eyes to say something else. The supervisor was suddenly wide awake, jumping all around and wringing his hands.

"No, it's okay, Pablo. We're really sor—"

"No, we're not," I interrupted. "Is this his last stop this morning?"

"Uh, yes."

"Good." I took out my pocket knife and slit the disposal bag, the inner one that contained all the dust and debris, and dumped it all onto the pavement.

Amidst the gray silt and finer particles that formed a cloud over the pile I had made were a dozen or so lumpy objects. I picked one up and blew it off, revealing a large silver and turquoise ring. The other objects were rings also, or bracelets or pendants. All told, about $1,000 in Indian jewelry.

"This is some machine," I mused. "The one I have at home won't pick up anything larger than a booger."

"I swear, I know nothing about this," Pablo protested, his tune and lyrics having changed abruptly.

"Can it, Pablo," I said. "And just for the record, where I was watching you from, I couldn't tell what race you were. I didn't accuse you because you were Mexican, I accused you because you're a crook! You give all the hard-working people from south of the border a bad name." I turned to his supervisor. "Well, Dan, what are you going to do with him? Shall I cuff him?"

"Please, no, sir," Pablo begged. "I have a wife and three kids —"

It was too early in the morning for this drivel. I stood up, dropping the jewelry into the pocket of my heavy black nylon coat.

"I'll write a report," I told Harris, "and send a copy to you and to my supervisors. Pablo's your problem."

I knew the park wouldn't prosecute. They'd notify his company; he'd be fired or perhaps only relocated to another customer's site — one where they had products that wouldn't fit inside vacuum bags. There'd be no turning this over to the police, no search warrant on his house, no recovery of the property he'd already stolen for who knows how long. Prosecuting criminals was bad

PR, and the park had had enough of that lately.

"The jewelry'll be locked in evidence," I told the janitorial supervisor. "In fact, why don't you and Pablo come with me to security. We'll lock it up together; then I'll have him escorted off the property. We can do that, at least, can't we?"

"Uh, yes, I suppose so . . ."

"Come on then. You, too, Pablo. Grab your stuff. You're finished."

The janitor picked up his gear without comment and followed me in silence.

I was reaching for the handle on the gate to go backstage when it suddenly swung open right at me. I drew my hand back just in time, only to be run into bodily by a rushing Dave Whelan, Manager of Ride Operations and Maintenance.

"Whoa!" I exclaimed as I grabbed his arms for support.

"Oh, sorry," he apologized, flustered. "You okay?"

"Yeah, Dave, I'm fine. What's the rush?"

"Oh, Beckman. Good morning. Didn't see you."

"I hope not. I'd hate to think you did that on purpose."

He laughed uncomfortably, the recent near-tragedies on his rides having drained the humor completely from him. I think he feared losing his job.

"So what's the hurry?" I asked.

"Nothing," he said hastily. "No hurry. You know how it is around here. Jerry wants this, the owners want that . . ."

"Usual stuff, then, I take it."

He nodded, wiping the sweat from his forehead with a handkerchief and stuffing it into the inside pocket of his double-breasted suit coat.

"Sorry again, Gil," he said. "Gotta go. See you around."

"Okay, Dave." Poor guy. I thought he was being set up to take the fall for Jerry for all the fiascoes around here, but there was no way to tell. I pressed on to security.

By the time Pablo had been walked to his car by a couple of day shift officers, Harry Clark had arrived, and I was sitting in his office, briefing him.

"How did you know it was in the dust bag itself?" he asked.

"When I was feeling around, I felt a small tear," I told him, "near the top and on the back side, where it might've gone unnoticed. There wasn't any loose dirt in the outer bag, so I knew the hole was new. It was the size of jewelry."

"Well, good job, Gil. Again. You know, I've never said this to you before, but you're really wasting your talents here."

"I've always thought that," I said, eyeing Harry out of the corner of my eye. "Actually, I seem to be using them, unless by 'wasting them' you mean I'm not being paid what they're worth."

Harry grinned sheepishly. "Yes, that's what I mean."

"So where do you suggest I go?"

"I — I don't know. I just think a man of your . . . experience ought to be doing something . . . else."

"What about you?" I asked. "That might apply to you too."

"Not really," Harry admitted. "In the first place, I have retirement pay coming in. Second, even though I was a cop, I was an administrator, and that's what I'm doing here at the park. And, to be quite candid, they pay me very well."

"What are you trying to tell me, Harry?"

"Uh, nothing r-really. It's j-just . . . Look, I feel bad that I — that *we* had to put you back down to officer. You're more valuable than that."

I'd been waiting two years for this opportunity. I leaned forward, resting my forearm on his desk. "Then promote me, Harry.

You're the boss — you have the authority."

He looked away, his fingertips drumming. "It's beyond me, Gil. That's all I can say."

I leaned back. I wasn't stupid, but it had taken quite an effort just for Harry to admit what he had. I wouldn't push him to the edge by pressing him to clarify exactly who was giving him his orders. Besides, it was obvious, at least to me.

"I understand, Harry. Maybe I'll give it some thought. You're probably right, I have no future here. But I'm okay right now. My needs aren't great. And after all, I had quite a bit of fun this past year, you've got to admit."

"You know . . ." he started, then motioned for me to close the door, which I did. When I sat back down he continued, "I put in for a bonus for you. Sort of a finder's fee, like insurance companies offer, for the return of the bullion. I mean, you've saved the park so much, it's the least they can do."

I was too stunned to respond. Which was okay, because he wasn't through.

"But it has to be approved by Opperman. I haven't heard anything about it — and it's been a couple of months — so I figure it's a dead issue. He probably figures the increase in your pay while you were working with Michelle was bonus enough. But I didn't want you thinking nobody noticed."

Shoot. No sooner do I see a ray of hope than a dark cloud zooms in to obliterate it. I smiled. "That's okay, Harry. It's good to know you tried at least. Maybe if I hadn't called Opperman an idiot, it might have been different."

"You called Jerry an idiot?"

"Not in so many words exactly. But even Jerry Opperman could understand my innuendo."

Harry smiled, and my respect for him grew because it was a wry smile that said he agreed with me even though he'd never put it into words. So he wasn't entirely a bad guy after all. Just a low-grade politician.

I stood. "Well, I've a vacation to get busy with," I said, glancing at my watch.

"Going fishing, I hear."

"Yep. Gonna fish, read, relax . . . The only effort I'm going to exert will be casting my rod and putting another log on the fire. I may not even eat unless someone else cooks. Except for Pop Tarts. I'll eat those. And if I find a dead body, I'm going to step over it and keep on walking."

Harry shook his head. "That'll be the day."

THREE

Sally Foster was in her office, and I popped in to say good-bye. "I feel bad, leaving you here," I told her.

"No, you don't," she teased.

"Yes, I do, actually," I asserted. I thought of saying something smart, like *I'll have to bait my own hooks or cook my own meals* but thought better of it and kept my mouth shut. Instead I said, "I enjoy your company."

"Well, thank you," Sally said quietly, dropping her head and looking down slightly as she smiled in that shy way of hers. "Maybe next time Estelle Curran and I can go too."

"You like fishing? Rachel always . . ." I faded out as soon as I caught myself talking about my deceased wife.

"That's okay, Gil," Sally said compassionately. "She was your wife, and you loved her. You don't have to forget her or even pretend that you've forgotten her."

"I'm sorry." I tried to sort out my thoughts. "I just thought it'd be best if I don't keep bringing her up around you."

"That's not what I said, Gil." Sally's voice was soft, without any hint of accusation. "I

45

said you need to stop doing things based on her memory or whether or not she'd approve. We can't have a relationship if you're going to feel guilty when you're with me, as though she's still alive. And when you have to keep catching yourself from mentioning her, that tells me she's still too fresh on your mind."

"No, she isn't," I defended. "I'm just trying to be sensitive to you, that's all — to your needs and feelings."

"Thank you, Gil, I appreciate that." Sally took a sip of hot tea from a delicate cup, one I'd given her. I bought it in Little Tokyo when I was walking around the area during the Hiromoto affair, as I had taken to calling it.

She continued, "Just be yourself, Gil, that's all I ask. If Rachel's memory keeps us apart, then so be it. Don't force it, please. But don't be afraid of commitment, if that's what you have in mind."

"It is. You know it."

She nodded. "I feel the same way, but only when you're ready. I believe God brought us together."

"So do I," I admitted. "But your husband treated you like so much baggage. He didn't care about you, just himself. It's easy for you not to think about him."

"Just because he did those things to me doesn't mean I loved him any less, you know." Sally's eyes moistened. "But that's over now. After he divorced me, I still held on to the hope that he'd come back."

"Would you have taken him back?"

"Yes, of course. It's what we Christians are supposed to do. And I would have, up until he remarried. That's when the hope died, and I prayed that God would heal the wound, help me close that chapter of my life. I still remember the good times though. But those memories don't run my life. They're just pictures in an album."

"It's different with Rachel. She didn't divorce me."

"No. She died. She left you without any hope, and with your heart unscarred and on fire for her. But she's gone just the same."

I hated conversations like this, especially when the things people said were right. I couldn't respond.

"Gil, look at me," Sally ordered sweetly. "I love you, Gil. Your warped sense of humor, your occasional bullheadedness, even your dogmatic opinions."

"I'm not dogmatic, I'm antithetical." She stared at me, and I grinned. I'd explain it to her some other time. "I'm sorry. Go on. You were telling me how much you love me."

Sally smiled. "But like I told you, I can't compete." There was no harshness in her words.

I nodded. "I hear you. And I love you too. I'm trying to figure this out. I want to do things right. I don't want Rachel's memory to get in the way, but I also don't want to . . ."

"You don't want to lose it either?"

"That's not really what I was getting at," I said. "It just came out that way."

"Go fishing, Gil. Think about it while you're wrestling a big one into the boat. I'll not make any demands on you, no ultimatums. And you don't have to choose between us. I just won't share you, that's all."

"That sounds like an ultimatum."

"I know," she admitted. "I didn't mean it to. But I think it's fair to expect . . . Let me put it this way, then I'm done: remember Rachel, respond to me."

I studied her face — plain but attractive, petite features, clear piercing eyes . . . I couldn't lose this woman. I needed to immerse myself in her, let her presence force Rachel into the background. Maybe Sally was right — I needed to make a commitment. My problem was, I was afraid to. What if I couldn't carry it off?

Time. I needed some time. Fortunately, I

48

was about to get some.

"Okay, Sal. Well, Harold and Joey are probably waiting. I'd better go." I leaned over to give her a kiss, and she hesitated — just to mess with my mind, I'm sure — then puckered up.

"Rachel who?" I said teasingly after a wet lip-lock. I turned to leave.

"Don't forget Mrs. Potter," Sally called after me.

I stuck my head back in. "Huh?"

"Mrs. Potter. I saw a note in dispatch. She wanted you to stop in before you left."

I snapped my fingers. "Oh, yeah. Thanks. I'd forgotten. Bye, Sally. I'll bring you a nice trout."

"Thanks just the same," she said, screwing her face up. "Just come home in one piece. See you next week."

I waved and walked away. Just come home in one piece? What could happen on a fishing trip?

Mrs. Potter's office — the administration office, since she was the secretary to the park's president — was a short walk away. It was an old building and housed Design and Planning, Food Services, some unmarked shops, and the formerly secret warehouse Sally and I had discovered some time back that contained all the artifacts and historical treasures the founder had collected over the years. But it was soon to be emptied now that the new museum being built on the property was almost finished.

The administration building wasn't just old; it was one of the first structures built on the property by the founder, Old Man Golden. Originally an assembly plant for some kind of light machinery, during World War II it was used to manufacture materials for the armed services. Secret stuff, so the rumor had it. Maybe helmets or machine guns or something. Whatever it was, Mr. Golden made his fortune on it, and a few years after the war ended, he was able to convert the plant and surrounding property into an amusement park — at taxpayer expense, so to speak. In fact, I'd noticed that a couple of backstage buildings were quonset huts, probably bought for a couple dollars from Uncle Sam and trucked here, just as the buildings of Manzanar, the Japanese Relocation Center in eastern California, had been sold for something like fourteen dollars each to returning servicemen. Many of them are still private residences, gas stations, and motels today.

The administration office had a long, dark porch added onto it, providing shade and a pleasant, laid-back feeling, with potted plants and a porch swing and rocking chair for people to use while waiting for an audience with the president. Jerry Opperman's parking place was empty, but it was only 8:30. An elderly man in a park maintenance uniform was rearranging the dirt on the asphalt with a hose, the potted plants and wet porch announcing that he'd just finished watering them. He was one of those guys who'd been with the park since day one, pulling down a good salary without having to actually do anything.

"Morning, Pop," I greeted as I skirted around the stream of water spewing from his hose.

"Whoa, almost got you there, Mr. Beckman," Al "Pop" Miller said with a wave. "Best watch out, I'm liable to soak you down!" I smiled appropriately. He returned to his duties, and I kept him in the corner of my eye as I passed. You could never tell with some people. He might have meant it.

I stepped onto the porch and entered the office, expecting to find Mrs. Potter at her desk. It was unoccupied, however, and appeared untouched, as though no one had been in that morning. I checked my watch again. She wasn't one to be late. Besides, wasn't she here when she left the message that she wanted to see me? Maybe she was in the back or with Opperman, wherever he was. I checked the desktop, but there was no note.

"Hello?" I called expectantly, hoping she'd hear. When there was no response, I poked my head around the corner and called again.

"Mrs. Potter, it's Gil. Gil Beckman." Still no answer. "Come out, come out, wherever you are." Jerry's door was shut, so I knocked lightly, paused, then banged on it several times. "Hey, Dragon Lady!" If that didn't raise her, she wasn't here. She'd earned the nickname by being a no-nonsense type of secretary who was very protective of Mr. Golden. In truth, she was a sweetheart, but that was a well-kept secret.

There was no response to my banging or my name-calling. Nothing but the hum of the air conditioning unit. Oh well, I had to get going, couldn't keep Harold and Joey waiting. I sighed and headed for the door, a little irritated that she made an appointment and didn't keep it herself. Then I remembered who she worked for — Jerry Opperman, Mr. Capricious, King of the Dipsy Doodles — and figured he'd probably come up with something for her to do and didn't care about her appointments. Of course, she might not have told him about me coming by either. The mere mention of my name made Jerry's face start to twitch.

I trudged out toward the employee parking lot, stopping to say hi to the receiving gate guard. As I left him, a black Mercedes pulled into the drive and came to a stop just shy of me. The tinted windows were all up, and as the driver's window began to slide down, I instinctively reached for my jar of Grey Poupon. Alas, I was on foot.

"Good morning, Miss Yoko—" I started to say, for it was her car, but I stopped short when the ugly mug of the driver came into view. It certainly wasn't the porcelain-skinned Japanese lady who was senior vice president of the park, second in command to Opperman, but rather the rough, rugged, and lined face of Lt. Theo Brown.

"Boy, the police department is going first class these days," I noted with a whistle. "Either that or you're taking freebies to a new level."

"Good morning to you, too," the lieutenant greeted dryly.

Michelle Yokoyama leaned over from the passenger seat so I could see her.

"Hello, Gil."

"Oh, hi, Michelle. Didn't see you behind the chauffeur."

"Keep it up, Beckman," Theo said.

"Thank you, but I generally don't need encouragement."

"Don't we know."

"Going on your vacation then?" Michelle queried politely. She knew I was. We'd discussed it when I was, shall we say, demoted a week before. The vacation was part of the deal. I think she was just trying to play referee. "Fishing, isn't it? Near Glenville, right?"

I nodded. "Dove Lake."

"That's a coincidence," she said. "Kumi Hiromoto told me he was going up that way once he wrapped up his work here, before returning to Japan."

"The deal go through then?"

"Looks that way. Everything's done but the final signatures. He'll probably bring us to Japan for that. He's very gracious."

"So what's he going to do up at Glenville? Fishing?"

"Perhaps," Michelle speculated. "But primarily I think he wants to visit Manzanar. He hasn't been back since he was shipped to Tule Lake. Kind of a pilgrimage, I suppose."

"Closure," I suggested. "Like visiting the scene where a loved one died."

"Perhaps. Maybe you'll see him at the lake."

"Maybe," I said, "if I can get out of here without finding a dead person."

"Please try," Theo said. "I'm beginning to suspect you might be killing them just so you can find them."

"Like the fireman with a pocketful of matches and nothing to do?" I asked. "Well, think about it — if I was going to do that, there are a couple of people I'd have already gotten to."

"Speaking of Captain Fitzgerald," Theo said without a second thought, "you pretty much managed to upset the whole department. What were you thinking?"

I shrugged. "Sorry. By the time I realized it was him, it was too late. I was committed. So how's the ol' boy doing?"

"Fifteen years as a cop, and you finally save someone, and you pick Bill. He's not too good, but he'll pull through. Be a while before he's back to work though."

"See there?" I said in my defense. "I didn't save him too good. Just enough. He's in a lot of pain then?"

"I'm afraid so."

I gave Theo a sorrowful look, then broke into a grin and rubbed my hands together.

"You know," Theo said thoughtfully, "perhaps I should check your CPR card. If it's expired, I'll have to run over to the hospital and unplug him so somebody who's certified can save him and make it valid."

"What's the penalty for saving a life without a valid card anyway?"

"You have to be his friend forever."

"I'll take death by torture, thank you."

"Are you two sickos about done?" Michelle asked dryly.

"Sorry, Michelle," Theo said, using her first name in front of me for the first time that I could recall. "See you later, Gil. Enjoy the fishing."

"You like to fish, Theo. Why don't you go?" I said. "Come on, you've got vacation time coming."

"Yes," Michelle agreed heartily. "That's an excellent idea!"

"Well, I —"

"Seriously, Theodore," I said. "What's so important that you can't take a week off? You think the department will grind to a halt without you there? Good grief, you're a lieutenant. You'd be missed just slightly less than Captain Whatshizname, which is zero."

"I guess I could do it . . ."

"Be assertive. Head on back and fill out the request, then approve it yourself. You're in charge of the division, the captain is gone, and the chief . . . Well, he's probably playing golf. Guaranteed, they won't miss you."

"What's that supposed to mean?" Theo asked.

"Yes," Michelle ordered, "do it. The rest will do you good."

"What's *that* supposed to mean?" Theo asked again with more emphasis, this time directing the question to Michelle.

"It means we love you," I told him.

Theo gave Michelle one of his *are you nuts?* looks. "Rest? You've obviously never gone fishing with Gil."

"No, I haven't," Michelle admitted. "But I imagine it's an experience."

"And the award for understatement of the year," I pronounced, "goes to —"

"It's settled then," she concluded. "Turn the car around, Teddy."

Theo's face blanched, then reddened, starting at the neck and moving slowly up his face like a thermometer in a pan of hot water. I grinned but said nothing. This was too delicious to waste now. Like the last chocolate in the box, I'd save it for later.

"Meet me at the Currans'," I told him. "We'll wait, but don't dilly-dally. The fish are calling."

Theo said nothing as his window glided up. He drove around the guard shack and headed for the street and the P.D.

I don't remember the first few hours of the drive. Once I got to the Currans' and stowed my gear in the back of Harold's new pickup and we waited for Theo to do the same, I was zombied out. Harold Curran was happy to have Theo along, as I knew he would be. Joey Duncan, the former juvenile delinquent turned park cartoonist, was a bit disconcerted, but the excitement of the trip soon took over, and the three of them chatted happily. I climbed in the back, under the color-matched camper shell, curled up on the sleeping bags, and fell immediately asleep.

When I woke up, we were pulling into a parking lot in some small town somewhere. I sat up, still groggy, and tried to focus.

"Good afternoon," Hal greeted me through the sliding rear window as Joey opened it.

"What day is it?" I asked, wiping my face with my hand.

"Same as when we left, but much later."

"I hate graveyard," I muttered.

"What do you mean, you hate graveyards?" Joey asked.

"Not graveyards," Theo explained. "Graveyard, as in the all-night shift. It's hard staying awake at his age."

"You made up for it," Hal said as he pulled the crew cab pickup into a parking stall.

"Yeah," parroted Joey. "You snored so loud, we could hear it through the window. We couldn't hear ourselves think."

"You didn't miss much," I replied. "Where are we?"

"Best breakfast cafe on the planet," Hal answered.

Theo turned around to look at me. "You've got a bad case of pillow hair, Gil. Comb it or put on a hat — we're going into a public place."

We piled out and stopped to stretch, and I obliged them by sticking my cowboy-style straw fishing hat — complete with state fishing license pinned to the front of the crown — on my disheveled head. I stretched and let my bones slip back into place. Sleeping in a vehicle had intensified the aches and pains acquired in recent weeks.

Following my fellow vacationers into the pancake house, I shook out the kinks and spun my head around a few times. The air was crisp, smog-free, and breezy, the sky azure with scattered puffy white clouds moving rapidly to the north, our intended destination. If they didn't rise a little higher, they'd stack up against the mountains, mingle, and — as is so common where we were headed — turn dark and serious. A clear, still morning could become an ugly, rainy afternoon.

The aroma inside the pancake house revived me. There's no better food on earth than a big stack of buttermilk pancakes soaked with maple syrup, with a side of steak and eggs, country fries, hot coffee . . . I think the manna God sent to the Hebrew children six mornings every week for forty years during their wandering in the desert was pancake fixin's. I don't have a Scripture verse to support my theory, but there's not one to prove me wrong either.

The decor of the restaurant was utilitarian, perfectly suited to travelers, families on vacation, fishermen, and campers seeking a last meal before having to eat canned food cooked out of doors. What was unique about the place were the mounted fish adorning the walls all around the large room. Twenty-six-pound brown trout, looking more like their cousins, chinook salmon, than they did the little things I was used to jerking out of the water.

Each plaque had a brass plate under the whale, engraved with the weight, date of catch, location, and the angler lucky enough to be holding the pole at the time God hooked the fish. I stared at one, drool dribbling out of the corner of my mouth and down my chin as the name on the plate faded out and back in again, only now it was my name, and the date was . . . tomorrow. Then the fish began to look like a grinning Jerry Opperman, and I shook the daydream off.

Taking my seat in the booth next to Theo, we scanned the menus and chose our poison. The waitress was quick with mugs of coffee and a Coke for the kid, and before long our stacks of pancakes and required side dishes had been set steaming before us.

"Eat hearty," Hal urged. "Might be the last good meal you get for a week."

We obeyed.

The highway climbed a seven-mile grade — the kind of grade that makes underpowered cars slow to twenty and motor homes overheat, the kind of grade that gets a name — while we watched the scenery change from high desert to high plains, from cottonwoods and Joshua trees to pine trees, from sagebrush and sand to sagebrush and sand and more sagebrush, from miles of nothing in all directions to miles of mountains in an upward direction.

Rugged, rocky, purple, amber, and gray, the Sierra Nevadas were magnificent mountains. Snowcapped virtually year-round, forbidding at their worst, sentinels of solitude when you stopped the car, shut off the engine, and walked away from the highway. And hidden in their many folds and valleys were untold numbers of small, natural lakes, all of them teeming with trout — maybe even some twenty-six-pounders.

And some of them had my name on them. Wait a minute, they *all* had my name on them.

I snickered out loud to myself.

"You okay, Gil?" Hal asked over his shoulder without taking his eyes off the road.

"He amuses himself all the time," Theo said laconically. "Ignore him."

"That's kind of hard, with all those quirks he has," Joey pointed out.

"This is a nice truck," I told Hal. I could have said a thing or two about Joey's quirks — like spray-painting anything that didn't move — but he hadn't done any graffiti since he found an outlet for his artistic urges. "When did you get it?"

"Couple weeks ago," Hal explained. "Paid cash for it. The park gave us a royalty check for Everett's ideas. Wasn't that nice?"

"Just peachy," I sulked, thinking back on Harry's revelation about a bonus for me that didn't go through. But I added quickly, lest

I sound too negative, "That's great, Hal. What'd you get for Estelle?"

"Let's see," he pondered, "new vacuum, new mixer, new lawn mower . . ."

"You better be kidding," Theo cautioned with a laugh.

Hal chuckled. "I am. She said she didn't want anything right now, so we put the rest in savings, to help with our retirement. She let me get the truck because she knew how long I've wanted one. I protested, of course —"

"I'll bet," Joey, Theo, and I said all at once.

We enjoyed a good laugh. Then conversation lagged for a moment. Joey picked it up again with a question out of the blue.

"What's an airport doing out here?"

I looked out his side of the truck and saw what he did.

"They decided to build it there because that's where all the planes kept landing," I told him.

"Oh," said Hal, "that's so all the rich folk can have easy, quick access to their vacation homes, and so people can go skiing without having to drive up like we did today. See all those cars behind the hangars? They leave them here, so when they fly up they can just land and drive away to their

63

condos. Pretty neat, huh?"

"Decadent," I said, knowing full well I'd do it if I could afford it.

"Must be nice," Joey agreed.

"Yeah," said Hal. "But not many people have the dough for that. Besides, all it saves you is a few hours' drive. And that's half the fun of the trip."

The rest of us gazed at Hal as if he'd just pronounced Jerry Opperman a good candidate for Pope.

"Look there, guys," Hal said, pointing. "Plane coming in."

"Oooh. I've never seen a plane land," Joey mocked.

"He's not only seen them land," I said, "he's painted his moniker on them as they went by." I watched the twin-engined Piper Seminole touch down lightly, then taxi over to a waiting vehicle, a Land Rover with some kind of emblem on the door. In fact, I now noticed the same emblem on the tail of the plane, though from this distance I couldn't make out what it was.

"Speaking of painting," Hal said to Theo and me in the backseat, "did you two notice what Joey painted on the side of my camper shell?"

"Do you want to prosecute?" Theo asked.

"Oh my, no," Hal laughed. "He painted

Everett the Dinosaur."

"Yeah," Theo said. "I saw it."

"Pretty neat, huh?"

It was. Everett the Dinosaur, the little mascot of the park that Hal and Estelle's son, the late Everett Curran, had designed, along with new rides and other attractions and merchandise. Joey, who now worked in Design and Planning at the park doing nothing but drawing the dinosaur, had painted the little guy smiling and waving, doing it with an airbrush in fine detail. A nice tribute, I thought. Joey's idea too. Maybe he was growing up at last.

"Are we there yet?" Joey whined.

Then again, maybe not.

"Half an hour," Hal said. "There's the road into the mountains." He turned off the highway. "Straight ahead a few miles is Glenville, the county seat. We'll turn off before we get there."

"Would it be too much of a hassle to stop in town first?" I asked. "Couple things I want to pick up." Like some junk food and a western novel."

"No problem," Hal assured. "It's not far."

"There's no snow," Joey observed as we wound our way up and into the trees.

"Not here," Hal said. "But up on the slopes there is. You'll see when we get to town. They've started making it already. In another month or so they'll have their first real snow of the season, but they can't wait for that. Their economy is based on tourism, and most of that comes from the skiers."

"Via the hospital," I added.

FOUR

The scenery could only be described as majestic. The pine trees, blue sky, white clouds, a lone eagle soaring silently overhead, the color of the earth, the contrast of hue between rock and snow, the smells, the sounds. I completely forgot about the theme park but did remember Sally, wishing she could be here to enjoy this with me.

It was chilly but not overly so. With winter just around the corner, it was near the end of the fishing season. In a few weeks the lakes would begin to ice over.

We rounded a bend in the twisting, pine-lined mountain road, and a small town spread out ahead of us, nestled in a short, straight valley between mountain ridges. It was typical of such towns — older A-frame shops mixed with log homes, stucco offices, and at least one Scandinavian-appearing restaurant. We passed a sheriff's department vehicle parked in front of a small cinder block building with a gold six-point star painted on the street-facing window over the word SHERIFF. The marked unit was a dark green Jeep Cherokee, with a red and blue light bar. It had the same star on its front doors. No one was in sight.

I sighed to myself, thinking what a cool job it would be to work in a place like this. Nothing to do all day but drive around the countryside, absorbing the scenery, sucking in the clean mountain air, occasionally driving to some out-of-the-way fishing hole to check licenses and, finding no one there, grabbing my secret pole from the back of my four-wheel-drive cop car and catching a few trout — on my lunch hour, of course.

Hal pulled up at the market, and we piled out, surprised at the chill in the air we hadn't noticed from inside the truck — a sharp contrast to the warm air we'd encountered at the pancake house. I glanced at Theo and could tell he was thinking the same thing. Joey didn't seem to notice.

Inside, I picked up a couple boxes of Pop Tarts, some jars of bait and number 16 treble hooks, and a Stephen Bly western I'd never read, then got in line at the only check-out counter. I noticed Joey had snagged a large package of beef jerky and a few candy bars. Hal didn't get anything, and I figured he'd done all his shopping before he left, where the prices were lower. We'd all chip in at the end of the trip to evenly distribute costs.

Theo waited by the door, hands in his

pockets, surveying the scene. Very cop-like. As I was checking out, he glanced over and noticed a newspaper rack.

"Hey, Gil, pay for a paper for me, would you? Kindling."

I nodded, and the checker, a wisp of a girl with long, straight hair framing an expressionless yet pretty face, punched the additional twenty-five cents into the register keys. I noticed that Joey seemed to be studying the young lady. Undoubtedly a local, she was blue of eye, brown of hair, and appeared to be Joey's age. She wore a small *ichthus* fish on a fine gold chain around her neck. When she glanced up at Joey and saw him staring at her, she looked immediately back at her register but ventured a second look at the young artist a minute later. A self-conscious smile flickered across her face, brief but unmistakable.

"Sooo," I said to Joey, a little more loudly than necessary, "your gear all ready for your ascent up the rock face in a couple days?"

He glared at me with a slight turn of his head, as if to tell me he didn't need any help. My ploy worked, however, and she spoke to him.

"You're a mountain climber?" An interested smile revealed two rows of small white

69

teeth as she accepted the money Joey held out.

"Rock," he corrected quietly. It was the first time I'd ever noticed him to be shy.

"What's the difference?" she wondered.

I answered, "Rock climbers don't have Sherpas."

"Oh," she said, but her face betrayed her total lack of understanding. "Sounds exciting. I'd be afraid to try it."

"If you know what you're doing, it's perfectly safe — with the right equipment," Joey said glibly.

"Do you climb without using ropes or anything?"

"Only up roller coaster supports," I said.

She looked at me, then back at Joey as she handed him his change. "This your dad?" she asked him.

Joey sneered. "He thinks so. He's my rock climbing partner when he's not acting like a parole officer." She gave me a funny look, and I gave her a grin.

"I don't climb," I explained. "I watch, hold the ropes, and call the paramedics."

"My name's Joey," he told her as she handed him his bag of goodies with a tentative stare.

"Jessica." She glanced at me.

"Gil," I said. "Pleased to meet you. Seriously, do I look old enough to be his father? Don't answer that. And he's kidding about me being his probation officer. I'm really his therapist." I made circles around my ear with my index finger and stuck my tongue out of the corner of my mouth. "We thought the mountain air would do him good."

"Where are you guys from?" she asked slowly, as if she was afraid the answer might be Mars or the Twilight Zone. Joey told her, adding that we both worked at the theme park. This brightened her disposition considerably.

"So, where are you guys staying? Are you camping or what?"

Joey shrugged and looked at me.

"I wouldn't call it camping exactly. We have a cabin on Dove Lake. Very primitive, I understand."

"Hardly anyone goes up there," she declared. "Too out of the way."

"Perfect," I said.

"Yeah, perfect," Joey echoed sarcastically. "I'll bet it doesn't have mints on the pillows."

"I'll bet it doesn't have pillows," I said.

"Will you be back in town at all?" she asked, somewhat hopefully to my reckoning.

"I don't . . ." Joey started.

"When we get hungry," I said. "Come on,

I think I hear a fish calling me." I left the market and went to the truck, where Hal and Theo were waiting. Joey followed reluctantly, giving the girl a last glance that she answered with a smile.

"Kind of far to drive for a date," I told him as we settled in the truck. Joey didn't answer as Hal drove back through town and turned onto the road that led to the lake.

We drove for half an hour, seeing no other cars on the road. The trees were thick, and we couldn't see further than the next bend in the road. Then we went up a hill and around a corner, and a small valley opened up in front of us. The view was so breathtaking that Hal stopped the truck square in the middle of the road, and we all got out. Below us, in the center of the valley, was the lake, an even deeper blue than the sky, surrounded by trees, with a stark granite mountain serving as a backdrop.

"Is that what I'm going to climb?" Joey said, his eyes wide.

Hal laughed. "Not this trip. Randolph, my son, told me there's some good climbing on a hiking trail about a mile east of the cabin, but you can't see it from here. Some bluffs, pretty sheer, lead to a plateau."

"How high?"

"Couple hundred feet, according to Randolph."

"Doesn't sound like much of a challenge," I said dryly.

"Neither does fishing," Joey countered.

"I don't fish because it's a challenge," I explained. "I fish because it's relaxing."

"Well, let's git to gittin'," Hal said, returning again to the truck. I drank in one last look and followed, so glad to be on vacation and away from the hassle of the park I almost couldn't stand it.

The cabin was small, made from logs, the seams daubed with some white stuff to keep out drafts. A rough, thick door hung in the opening facing the road. The thick shake roof was covered with moss, the fireplace made of river stones, gray and black; the windows, of which there were two flanking the door and one on the end that was facing us, were set in with glass panes. The shutters were open, and red and white curtains provided the privacy we wouldn't need, unless you consider bears and squirrels nosy neighbors.

The cabin was rustic with a capital rust. But I loved it. I'm not so sure about Joey. He had that look of disdain with which one regards a plate of broiled roaches or a glass of curdled milk.

"This place has cable, right?" he asked, hope springing eternal.

"We did," Hal said with a grin. "Nintendo too. And a microwave oven, VCR with a 300-tape library. Had it all moved out last week to make room for your bed."

"Bring it back. I'll sleep on the floor."

"What floor?" I asked, opening the back of the camper shell to unload the gear.

"What do you mean, what floor?"

"What do you mean, what do I mean? This cabin doesn't have a floor. Other than dirt, at least. I bet it's not that different from your apartment."

Joey gave me a venomous look, then pushed the cabin door open slowly. It creaked on its hinges, very peaceful and natural sounding.

"It's dark," he complained. "Where's the light switch?"

"Right there on the wall," Hal said. "It's called a lantern. Just open the curtains. That'll be enough light for now. Let's get a fire going."

"Good idea," I agreed. "We can burn this cabin down and build a new one with electricity for Mr. City Pants."

I grabbed a couple armloads of stuff and followed Joey through the door. The cabin wasn't as bad as we'd painted it. It did indeed have a nice wood plank floor, covered by several of those oval braided cotton rugs and a large bearskin in front of the fireplace.

"Is that real?" Joey asked.

"Real dead," Theo told him.

"Don't the, uh, like, animal rights people get upset?"

"We don't let them stay here," Hal said. "Besides, this here bear was asking for it. He raided the cabin one night. Ate three campers before we could take him out."

I set the stuff I carried on the dining table, hiding my grin from Joey. The kitchen, if it could be called that in this one-room lodge, had a sink with a pump handle and a wood-burning stove. Outside, around back on a pleasant little deck overlooking the lake, was a large propane barbecue with side burner where all our meals could be prepared.

Inside a cupboard was a small icebox, and Hal came in with an ice chest that contained a block of dry ice he'd brought with him. He gloved his hands and carefully lifted it into place. A second ice chest held the food, which he put in also. There appeared to be ample for our stay, and Hal pointed to a package wrapped in white paper.

"Dinner," he said, but would tell us no more.

Once everything was inside and we had claimed our respective cots, I took a walk down to the lake. The water was clear and smooth as glass. Birds chirped, a fish jumped, and all was right with the world.

Suddenly — and unexpectedly — Sally popped into my head, and I missed her. I thought about her, about being here with her, and wished she could have come. I didn't realize it until later, but Rachel didn't enter my mind.

Hal called from the cabin, "Gil, want to get some fishing in? Looks like a storm's brewing." He pointed east, toward the granite mountain. Indeed, dark clouds were creeping over the peak and rolling down.

"How long do we have?"

"Three, four hours. That's plenty of time. Be dark about that time too."

"You're on." I hiked back up to the cabin, and we gathered our fishing gear. "Boy, I'm starved," I said, grabbing a box of Pop Tarts. Hal brought a thermos of coffee he'd just fixed.

"How can you eat those?" Joey asked, unwrapping a candy bar.

"It's easy. I rip off the end of the package, reach in and extract a Pop Tart, put it into my mouth in bite-size segments, chew thoroughly, then swallow and keep doing it until it's all gone. Then I get another one."

"Come on, you know what I mean."

"Yeah, but I don't know why you ask. It's all a matter of taste, isn't it?"

"They don't have any taste. Good grief, you don't even toast them. Aren't they kind of doughy?"

I shrugged. "Never thought of it. I happen to like crust. That's the best part of a pie, don't you think, Hal?"

"No," he said.

"Whatever. There are some chips there if you want, Joey. Bring those."

He shrugged once and picked them up, along with some cans of soda. "We do have a boat, don't we?"

"Oh yeah," Hal said. "It's waiting for us at the dock. Randolph brought it up for us this morning."

We walked down to the water, stopping at the edge of the dock. There, tied with a thin rope, sat the worst-looking rowboat I'd ever seen. Maybe ten feet long, no paint left on it, the seat planks cracked, one oarlock missing, and the only remaining oar was split its entire length. And it was half full of water. Or half empty, depending on your outlook.

"I might have known," Joey said. "Fits the cabin perfectly."

I didn't say anything but cast Hal a furtive

glance out of the corner of my eye. He was smiling.

"It's over there," he said softly. "In those bushes."

Joey trotted over to investigate and returned sullen.

"What's the matter?" Hal asked. "Isn't it there?"

"Oh, it's there," Joey said. "But it's not much better than this." He jerked a thumb toward the *Leakin' Lena.*

"It's a brand-new fishing boat," Hal protested. "Fourteen foot, aluminum, five horse motor. What were you expecting?"

He shrugged. "I guess a boat like they have on those fishing shows on cable."

Theo told him, "Those low-slung, high-powered things are set up strictly for bass fishing."

"What's the difference? Fish are fish."

"No," I said. "Bass and trout are fished two entirely different ways. Bass fishing requires a live well so the fish don't die after you catch them, a trolling motor on the front with a foot pedal so you can sneak up to them in the trees, and a big ol' motor on the back so you can beat everyone else to the best hole after the starter's gun goes off. For trout you need a stick, a string, and some cheese on a safety pin. In other words, trout fishing is for people who can't afford bass boats."

Hal chuckled as he set his gear on the dock and plowed through the brush to bring the boat to us, but no sooner did he get it started than the clouds that were so far off suddenly tumbled in, letting loose as they came. We could see a wall of water moving swiftly toward us. So we tied off the boat and scrambled back to the cabin, latching the door securely behind us just as the deluge hit.

"There is a God," Joey mumbled.

"Three or four hours?" I cast Hal a skeptical, disdainful look.

He shrugged. "Give or take three or four hours. So sue me."

"I'm considering it." I turned to Joey. "I hope you're not, like, major disappointed or anything."

"I'm severely traumatized," he deadpanned, flopping onto his cot and opening a hot rod magazine.

"Lingo he picked up from his social worker in juvenile hall," I explained to Theo.

"Yeah." Theo peeled off his fishing vest. "I'm starved anyway. What's for dinner, Mr. Curran?"

"Please, Lieutenant, call me Hal."

"And Theo for me," Theo said.

Or Teddy, I thought to myself, but I didn't vocalize it.

"Well, I was actually planning on fish," Hal said, his face serious. "I hope you guys don't mind settling for steak."

A choir of three gave Hal a rousing cheer.

There is little better in life than steak, Tater Tots, a roaring fire, and rain on the roof. Only two things could have made the evening grander — the company of that special someone and a large hunk of deep-dish apple pie á la mode.

And Hal brought the pie.

After a meal like that, following a long day of driving, not to mention working graveyard the night before, we were exhausted. As the rain slacked off and the clouds broke to unveil a bazillion stars, we had little choice but to climb into our sleeping bags.

Theo and I spent the waning moments of our consciousness reading the newspaper he'd picked up in town, he with the sports page, me with the funnies. After the important stuff, I went on to the local news, to see whose prize jam won the blue ribbon at the county fair. The lead story surprised me.

"Hey, check this out," I said to Theo.

"What?" He set down the sports.

"Says here a local real estate agent, a female, was murdered the other day. Her body was found stuffed in the trunk of her car on a deserted road outside town."

"Pity," Theo said. "What time's reveille?"

"No, listen. It says Sheriff Thomas is stumped and is asking the public for help. We're public."

"No, we're not, we're tourists. Forget it, Gil. Now blow out the light, and go to sleep. You'll forget all about that when you're fighting the first seven-pounder."

I closed my eyes and imagined the fish. "Forget all about what?" I asked dreamily.

"That's more like it. Good night, Gil."

"Good night . . . Teddy."

I covered my head just in time to deflect the newspaper Theo threw. When the coast was clear, I peeked out, turned the lantern down, and snuggled further into my sleeping bag. Hal's peaceful, rhythmic snoring and the light patter of a dying rainstorm provided a good backdrop for nodding off, and as I listened to it I couldn't help but thank the Lord for His blessings in my life. I was having a great time so far. I had a decent job and was looking forward to my future with Sally Foster, whatever that might entail. God had even allowed me in recent months to do what I loved best — solve crimes.

I thought of Joey and Theo and prayed

that God would give me the privilege of helping them into the kingdom. Even as I was praying this, Theo called me quietly.

"You asleep?"

"Yes."

"I've been reading what you gave me." He paused.

"And?"

"And I've got some questions."

"Shoot."

"Not yet. I'm making a list. I want to get through the whole book."

"You're going to read the whole Bible before you ask a question?" Now that was dedication, I told myself. It shamed me. I couldn't honestly claim to have read the whole Bible. It's so easy to skim over the begats and the books of Numbers and Deuteronomy. And the prophets. And the —

"No, goofball, the book of John."

"Oh." Whew. I could repent of my previous repenting. "Well, let me know. I hope I can answer them when the time comes, or at least guide you to where you can find the answers."

"Yeah," he said, barely above a whisper. "Good night."

"See you in the morning. You too, Joey." The young man had been listening to us, which was okay with me.

"Huh? Oh, yeah. See ya."

I fell asleep that night with a prayer and a praise on my lips.

As we hiked down to the lake the next morning, I looked up at the moon, still visible just above the horizon. It was almost full.

"They probably won't be biting," I lamented to Hal.

"No, probably not," Hal agreed. "But we're going fishing, not catching. It's enough just to kick back in the boat, munch on junk food, and relax on a peaceful lake, even without a nibble, isn't it?"

Theo and I looked at each other. Then both of us answered simultaneously, "No!"

Joey had opted to stay at the cabin and keep the fire going while he readied his gear for the next day's climb. So Theo, Hal, and I loaded the boat and cast off, bailing a bit of water from the previous night's rain with the top of Hal's thermos. Two minutes later we were in position.

I broke open the chips as Theo made his first cast.

"Sure was nice of the girls to let us come up here, wasn't it?" Hal said, taking the bag from me and reaching in for a handful of breakfast.

"Yep, sure was," Theo agreed.

"How much did it cost you?"

"Seventy-five."

"You're lucky. Estelle wanted a hundred, plus fifty for gas money," Hal one-upped.

"What's this?" I asked. "You guys had to bribe the women to get permission? Hal I understand. But Theo? You're not even married."

"As good as," he said. "Can't wait until I am. Bet the price goes up."

"She makes more than you," I pointed out.

"Doesn't matter," Hal said. "You'll learn. If you don't take 'em with you, you gotta pay."

"Rach— I mean, Sally would never do that."

"Bet me," Theo said. "You'll find out soon — whoa, lookee here!" His rod tip began dipping. "Hey, I got one!"

Hal dropped the bag of chips. "I haven't even baited my hook," he complained.

"Easy now, not too fast," I instructed.

"Shut up, Gil, I know how to fish!"

"Let him get a good bite . . . Now!"

Theo jerked the pole so hard that he slipped off the back of the seat into the bottom of the small aluminum boat, crushing my food.

"Whoa! Hey, watch out!" I yelled. "What're you trying to do, jerk him clean out of the lake?"

"I've still got him!" Theo struggled with the pole.

"Get off my food — you're smashing it!"

"I can't. If I give him any slack he'll break my line!"

"Here, give me your pole."

"No, I'll bring him in."

"Not lying on my chips and cupcakes you won't!" I grabbed a knife from my tackle box and advanced toward Theo, now on his back fighting the rod and reel with his legs hung over the seat.

"Help me . . . Hey, what're you doing? Get away from my line!" Theo pulled himself up onto the seat and snatched the knife from my hand. "You're insane! What're you — whoa! Look at him jump!"

"Yeah, that's great!" I said. "That's — that's *my* fish! Look at my pole!"

I grabbed my rod just before it was dragged overboard. Now both of us struggled to reel in our catch.

"Get the net!" Theo yelled.

"Get it yourself. I'm busy!" I yelled back.

"I can't! It's out of my reach."

"Just a minute . . . I'm reeling in."

"Hurry up, I don't want to lose this one."

"Me neither!"

"C'mon!"

"Uh oh, he's going to your side."

"The lines are going to get crossed!"

"Watch it!"

"Move your fish!"

"How do I do that?"

"Pull him in."

"Pull yours in!"

"Look out! There they go!"

"Oh no, the lines are twisted."

"I have the net."

"Can you get them both?"

"I can try — uh oh, your hat! Sorry about that. It'll dry."

"If I can get it back."

"Watch it . . . watch it!"

"Got 'em!"

"Just in time. The lines broke."

"Both of them?"

"Yep. Look there . . . Yours is kinda small."

"Mine? Mine's the big one — yours is the small one."

"No way. I saw mine!"

"So did I. You were lying down, remember?"

We dumped the fish in the bottom of the boat and stared down at them as they flopped on the aluminum. Two beautiful rainbow trout, all of eight, nine ounces each, barely enough meat for a small boy. We admired the fish, grimaced at the mess they'd made of our boat, and watched Theo's hat float away.

"It doesn't get much better than this, old buddy," Theo grinned.

I nodded. "You said it, partner."

Six cupcakes, a bag of potato chips, four sandwiches, two dozen cookies, and several cups of coffee later, the three of us had settled down into the afternoon fisherman's lull. None of us had caught enough fish to bother firing up the grill, and the garbage we had eaten was gluing us to the bottom of the boat.

Nothing was biting now. The afternoon sun had been beating mercilessly until the clouds rolled in again about a half-hour before, and we were ready to go to sleep, so full of sugar and grease we felt like giant cream-filled sandwich cookies.

Theo dozed with his hat over his face, while Hal fussed with a reel. I watched the shoreline move rhythmically up and down in an almost hypnotic way (my eyelids were getting heavy — very heavy). The only sounds we heard were the waves slapping the sides of the boat, the cry of gulls flying overhead, the motors of other boats, the shouts of fellow fishermen, the not-too-distant thunder, the patter of rain on the tops of our heads . . .

Hal put down the reel and yanked the starter rope, making the motor sputter into life, then cranked the throttle wide open. The boat lurched toward the shore. Theo didn't budge.

"Moving to a better spot?" he mumbled, barely audible.

"No, I'm moving to a drier spot," Hal said. "I don't want to get caught out in this rainstorm. Looks like lightning."

"Mmmm."

"Sounds refreshing," I muttered.

"And we're in an aluminum boat," Hal clarified.

Theo and I both jumped up, leaned over the side, and began paddling furiously with our hands.

We made it to the dock just as the deluge hit, grabbed our gear, and retreated to the cabin, tossing everything into the corner as we headed for the fireplace . . . which Joey had let go out. The kid gave us a raised-eyebrow glance, then went back to whatever it was he was doing.

Undaunted, Hal built the fire anew while

I put on a fresh pot of coffee. Soon we were all sitting around some blazing logs, sipping the strong, steaming brew and silently watching the rain pour into the lake.

FIVE

After a light breakfast — light pancakes smothered with light butter and light syrup, with light sausage and light fried eggs on the side — Joey and I set out for our climb. His climb, actually. I could tell he was excited, even though his face and attitude didn't show it. It was his step; he was livelier than he'd been so far on the trip.

It was a good day for it too. The storm had passed, leaving everything clean and fresh, and there wasn't a cloud to be seen. The temperature promised to go up a few degrees.

"Okay," he said, "do you remember what I told you?"

"I think so," I said pensively, my fingers on my chin. "Keep the rope taut, and if you fall I'm not supposed to try to catch you."

"Funny."

"Relax, Joey, I remember. How far is this place anyway? I don't want to be all tuckered out before I even get there."

"Mr. Curran said it's just up the road about a mile, then left along a hiking trail. He said the trail's easy to spot, and we can see the cliff from the road." He shifted the large canvas bag that hung from his shoulder, causing a heavy metallic sound from the shifting gizmos inside — the carabiners, pitons, descenders, and flexible camming devices that would aid and protect him during his climb. He also carried two long, sheathed, nylon ropes, special shoes, and a small sack of resin powder for his fingers.

The bag I lugged contained lunch. It figured to be considerably lighter on the way home.

Actually, this was one of those hikes you don't really mind — a cool morning in the mountains with the sun on the rise, peeking through the abundant evergreens and orange aspens, the sky so blue you just have to stare, brilliant white clouds scattered here and there, moving swiftly in the high-altitude currents while the trees around you are still, even the delicate aspens, which yield to the slightest movement of air, a bag full of food to consume later while sitting on a moss-covered log . . .

A dead, decomposing log covered with moss and bugs, ants, spiders, grubs, termites . . . I'll eat standing up, thank you.

We found the trail easily, as Mr. Curran had said. Moving off the dirt road onto the trail as it disappeared into the undergrowth, we could see the cliff looming ahead through breaks in the trees. Joey stopped for a moment at one point, and — although I wouldn't swear to it — I think he was having second thoughts. But he let out a lungful and shifted his load to the other shoulder, as if to excuse his pause, and continued without comment. Even if he'd wanted to go back, he wouldn't. Not here, not in front of me.

At the base of the cliff was a clearing, and Joey dropped his bag and opened it. He removed a funny-looking pair of tennis shoes — climbing boots, actually. They were colorful canvas high-tops with black rubber soles that had no tread and came well up the sides, back and toe. Joey explained that the rubber was sticky, like racing car tires, and gave good traction even on rock with no footholds. I nodded knowledgeably, thinking there was no way on God's green earth I'd ever trust my life to a pair of tie-dyed tennis shoes.

"They look small," I noted, comparing them visually to Joey's regular sneakers.

"They're supposed to fit tight. Slop is your enemy."

"I've always believed that."

"You need to feel the rock with your toes. You can't dig in if there's room for the shoe to collapse in front of your toes."

He extracted a harness that he stepped into and velcroed tightly around his waist and thighs. From it he hung the cams and protection devices he'd need during his ascent and one of the ropes. He secured a carabiner — an aluminum alloy ring shaped like a *D* with a threaded sleeve — to a ring on the front of his harness. He slid a double-ring deal, in the shape of a figure eight with one ring larger than the other, onto the carabiner, and he then threaded the knurled sleeve down tight.

He was ready.

"Sure you don't want to go up?" he asked. "It's a lot of fun. You may never get another chance."

"Thanks but no thanks. I've had all the heights I can stand recently."

"Listen, Mr. Beckman, after your athletics on top of the roller coaster, this will be easy."

"As easy as falling off a cliff," I said. "*Terra firma* is my friend."

"Okay. You remember what to do, right?"

"Yes, Joey, for the fourth time I do."

"Okay. Just remember, until I get a ways up and get a chock secured, don't pull on the rope. I'll be free-climbing for the first ten, fifteen feet. Once I have some protection, if I slip, take out the slack like I showed you."

"I've belayed before, when I worked SWAT," I reminded him.

"I know. I'm just making sure. It's my neck, you know." He glanced at me, and I gave him a devilish grin, just enough to make him stop and think. But he was getting used to me and waved me off. He rigged a chock at the base of the cliff and ran the rope around me so if he fell, my hands wouldn't have to stop his weight all alone — my entire body would help.

Joey tied the other end of the rope onto his belt and left the bulk of it coiled by my feet.

"Okay, off I go."

"Okay," I repeated. "Have at it."

He began his ascent, climbing slowly but confidently, using foot- and handholds, pulling himself up by his fingertips, ramming a fist or a foot into a crevice or crack. The shoes were remarkable, allowing him to push up from a piece of rock sticking out a half-inch, if that. About fifteen feet up he stuck in his first chock, a metal hexagonal thing with a nylon strap attached. He hooked the rope onto it with a carabiner.

"Okay!" he shouted down. "I'm on! Tension!"

"Gotcha!" I called back as I took in the slack. Now if he slipped, he'd only fall as far as the length of rope between him and the nearest protection device — providing I belayed him properly. If I didn't, and he plummeted, I'd jump out of the way and turn my head.

Joey proceeded up the rock face cautiously, placing a new chock or hexcentric or a flexible friend — a cam device for larger cracks that gets tighter the more the rope is pulled — every fifteen feet or so. Occasionally he'd shout down "slack" or "tension," and I'd respond accordingly on belay. It was exciting watching him from a vantage point below. Although not exactly vertical, the cliff was nearly so, with an interesting assortment of feature variations — chimneys, ridges, cracks, ledges, aretes. It lacked an overhang, probably the toughest challenge in rock climbing, since it requires mostly fingers and arms, as there are no places for your feet until you're over the bottom edge.

He was fifty, sixty feet up when I heard a buzzing sound to my rear, quite a distance away. As it grew louder and presumably closer, I recognized it to be an airplane, a private prop job. Then I identified a sound that disturbed me. It was a twin, and one of the engines was faltering.

The plane drew closer, and even Joey stopped climbing and hazarded a look.

Maintaining proper tension on the rope, I looked too.

It was low, not all that far above the tree-tops, and it was losing altitude. Though not headed directly for us, it looked to be on a path for the top of the plateau we — or rather, Joey — was climbing toward.

As it flew over and to my left, the wings wobbling scarily, smoke billowed from the right engine. Then the plane crested the top of Joey's rock face and disappeared from our view. We could still hear it, though not as well, having lost line of sight — but enough to know it wasn't going to make it.

Seconds later that was confirmed as it sputtered and died. A few seconds of deafening silence were followed by the sickening strains of tearing, crushing metal and cracking wood. Then when all had settled, another silence, this one permanent. Even the birds were still.

Joey looked down. "What do we do now?"

"We need to report it," I yelled.

"But what if there are survivors?"

"Go on up, check it out," I urged.

A worried look creased his face. "I wouldn't know what to do. You come up too. What if I need help?"

I stared at him. "You're kidding. How?"

He thought, looked up the rock face, then

back down. "I'll go to the top, secure the rope, and belay you from there. I'll toss down the shoes and harness."

There was no way I was going to begin my rock climbing career with a climb like this. This was for people with experience — something I intended never to have.

Joey read my mind.

"You'll be okay!" he called. "There are plenty of foot- and handholds, and if you slip, the rope will hold you."

I thought of those people up there, probably dead. But there had been no plume of smoke that we could see, and by now it would be high enough to get a glimpse of it if the plane had caught fire or exploded. Could they have survived the crash landing itself? It was possible. Very possible.

Joey was right. I had to go up.

"Okay!" I shouted, wondering what I was getting myself into.

"Slack!" Joey yelled, and I let up a touch on the rope as he resumed his climb. I watched him carefully, trying to remember not only his route, but also where he'd found his hand- and footholds.

The emergency seemed to inspire Joey, and he completed his climb quickly, leaving me too little time to get overly apprehensive. He scampered over the top — not even tak-

ing time to revel in his accomplishment —
and tied off the rope, then called for me to
take in the slack. When I gave him a wave,
he shouted for me to watch out and dropped
the harness and shoes over the side. I slipped
them on, tied my own shoes over the harness
in the back where they wouldn't come between me and the rock, and started up, keeping my mind on other things, like Sally and
Jesus and dinner.

Joey kept up a constant patter of encouragement and instruction while using his
body to belay me, keeping the rope just slack
enough to make me feel confident in its
ability to stop me if I fell. The going wasn't
easy, nowhere near as easy at it looked when
Joey was doing it. I was scared, I'm not
ashamed to admit, and by the time I was
high enough to kill myself, my head was
swimming.

"Don't look down!" Joey shouted. I hadn't
been, and I had no intention of it. I was too
busy looking up, trying to turn my fingers
into large suction cups. If grabbing the wall
with my teeth would've helped, I'd have
done it.

I've watched guys on TV climbing like
this. I'd seen Stallone do it in *Cliffhanger*. It
looked easy — people scampering up sheer
rock faces with no protection devices, no

ropes, crawling like flies on the ceiling.

This wasn't like that. My muscles ached, the skin on my fingers was being rubbed off, my fingernails were ragged and broken, my knuckles were skinned, and the adrenaline was beginning to give me the shakes — not a good thing when you're hanging by your fingers and toes on a near-vertical rock face fifty feet from sudden impact.

"You okay?" Joey was calling down to me, but it took a second to register.

"Yeah," I fibbed. "Just planning my route."

"Kinda hard to do with your face sucking rock, don't you think?"

"I'm okay!" I told him, reminding myself that I was doing this for a purpose, not just to prove I could do it.

"Say, Joey!"

"Yeah? Something wrong?"

"No, I was just wondering . . . Why don't you just haul me on up?"

"Yeah, right. How?"

"I don't know. Tie me off to Trigger's saddle horn and have him back up."

"Funny. Come on, Mr. Beckman. Those people . . ."

I nodded and found a toehold by feel. I could see a crack about three feet up, large enough to cram my hand into. I tensed, pushed up with my legs, and stuck my fingers into it. They held, and I repeated the process with my other foot. With my thoughts trained on the people in the plane, and on God, whom I would meet face to face sooner than I intended if I wasn't careful, I kept going.

Just fifteen feet shy of the rim — which translated to roughly 185 feet from the ground — my worst fears were realized. I strained for the closest handhold I could see — a button of rock about the size of a pair of dice — with my right hand, pushing up with my toes, my left hand fisted into a vertical fissure. I grabbed the rock with my fingertips and withdrew my fist to grab higher as a surge of pride and accomplishment welled up inside me.

But it stuck in my throat as I saw my fingers pop off the granite knob, and for a split second I was grasping air. With just my feet keeping me on the rock, I felt gravity pulling me away from the cliff. In a slow, exaggerated motion, the rock wall receded, and I cried out. My hands grabbed desperately for the cliff, but I knew that even if I could reach it, I wouldn't be able to do much more than push myself further away.

I knew I shouldn't look down, that it would be the worst thing I could do, but I couldn't help it. I knew at that moment how people facing disaster feel, how they are drawn into whatever is about to destroy them, whether it be a fall into a deep canyon, a leap from a building, jumping from an airplane, being overtaken by fire, or being about to be eaten by Godzilla. They are fascinated with this ultra-powerful thing over which they have no control, which is seconds away from killing them, and yet they are so awed at how curious and wonderful it is, they just have to stare at it.

I've often wondered, why do skydivers whose parachutes fail to open kick and scream all the way down? Surely they realize nothing they can do will prevent them from slamming into the ground. They are going to die, so why not at least relax and enjoy the trip? If nothing else, in fact, above all else, take those last few moments to call on God.

The thought passed quickly, though, as I came to myself and realized I was indeed falling. I looked down, trying to pinpoint the spot where I'd land, expecting the ground to rise toward me in a hurry. But a sudden tightening around my waist and groin jerked my feet up above my head, my body slamming into the rock face, bouncing, coming to rest with my back against it, my head below my feet. White powdered resin fell from the inverted bag and dusted my face, then drifted downward in swirls on the air currents.

The words of a song flashed through my brain. *Can't keep my eyes from the circling sky, tongue-tied and twisted just an earth-bound misfit, I.*

Instinctively I clutched for the rope as I became aware that Joey was shouting at me, barely audible over the pounding of blood in my temples. I swallowed my heart as both hands strangled the rope, and I fought to right myself.

"Turn over!" Joey shouted.

"What do you think I'm trying to do?"

"That's it! Easy now . . . Pull hard . . . Hurry up . . . Not too quick!" His terse, somewhat contradictory directions helped me maintain my equilibrium as I hauled myself upright. I was next to the rock, and before I gave myself time to think about what had just happened, I found some toe- and fingerholds and repositioned myself on the cliff. Time was of the essence.

I had lost only about ten feet and quickly made that up again, reaching in only a few minutes the spot where I'd just fallen. This time, though, I looked to the right, then the left, and saw that my path should jog right before resuming vertical, as there were plenty of holds that way. I took a breath and eased myself across the rock, ignoring my bleeding fingers, pulsating temples, and muscle spasms that threatened to knot up my calves.

I climbed two feet, with my right fist shoved into a wide crack and my left foot pushing from a one-inch ledge, then re-gripped, pulled up, moved my other foot into the crack vacated by my fist, pushed, reached, crammed, pulled, stretched, groaned, prayed, breathed, tightened the rope, heard Joey's shouted encouragement, twisted, shoved, pulled, pushed, gripped . . . A hand reached out to me, and I grabbed the wrist as Joey grabbed mine. Suddenly I was kneeling on the top, then standing on shaking legs, and we hugged. A Kodak moment if ever there was one.

It was over. I had conquered the mountain.

Okay, it was just a little cliff. But at that moment, if I'd had the time, I'd have raised my arms with fists clenched and turned to face the edge and danced to the theme from *Rocky*.

But it was all I could do to stand there and take off the harness and those horrendously uncomfortable climbing shoes.

I looked off through the forest.

"Where is it? Could you tell?" I asked Joey while struggling with my shoelaces. Easy tasks become difficult when your hands are shaking uncontrollably.

"That way," he said, nodding. "No idea how far."

"Let's get to it then."

Leaving the gear concealed in some bushes — purely out of habit, I suppose, like we really expected a thief to happen by — we took off at a trot in the direction Joey thought the plane had gone down. A trot isn't a literal description. My legs were barely supporting my weight, much less taking me along in a hurry.

"Here," Joey said after a few minutes.

He was holding something out to me — one of those protein bars. Chewy, faintly reminiscent of food, but full of untapped energy just waiting to explode into my system and set my extremities spinning, like Popeye's arms after he sucks a can of spinach through his pipe.

And it was just what the doctor ordered. Joey also produced a small bottle of one of those sport drinks, from where I didn't notice, which we shared.

"What?" I asked. "No Pop Tarts?"

"Those sap your strength," he said.

"Nonsense. Besides, they taste better than this chewy cardboard."

"I'm serious," he said. "Every time you eat one of those things, you go to sleep."

"That's only because I eat them when I'm doing something that's relaxing anyway. Like fishing."

"Well, even so —"

We broke into a clearing and stopped, seeing our objective at the same instant. Not the plane itself, but the obvious path of the plane on the far side of the clearing — a path through the trees cut by the wings as it failed to land where the pilot had been aiming but instead continued into the forest on the far side of the meadow.

I started to run but couldn't maintain the pace. The spirit was willing, but the flesh was weak. Without comment Joey ran ahead and disappeared into the trees before I'd traversed half the distance. When I made it, huffing and puffing, I called Joey.

He shouted back, "Keep coming! It's fifty yards in!"

I pressed on, and soon the plane came into view. It was upright, both wings sheared off and lying bent and broken to the sides of and behind the fuselage, which had plowed a furrow in the forest floor and was nose-down in the dirt, the nose cowling of the aircraft partially buried, the tail suspended a couple feet off the ground. There was no smoke or flame coming from the wreckage, the detached engine pods were more or less intact on their wings, and all was eerily peaceful. The sunlight filtered through the trees in shafts, illuminating the dust that still floated over the scene.

Joey stood by the starboard passenger door, which had been opened and nearly ripped off by the impact. Judging by the way he stared, his mouth open, eyes fixed and wide, I knew.

I put my hand on his shoulder and peered in. The pilot was dead, with obvious wounds to his face and chest that best remain undescribed. The man next to him, closest to us, was also clearly beyond help.

I craned my head to see into the rear seats. A man and a woman were there. He was slumped forward on the far side, his wound invisible to me at the moment. The woman was bleeding from a cut on her head and was sitting back, her mouth open and bleeding, her eyes glazed.

She gurgled, trying to breathe.

"She's alive," I told Joey. "We have to get her out of there."

I reached in and unbuckled the seat belt of the man in the front passenger seat, then grabbed him around the chest and dragged him outside. When his body was clear of the plane, it was obvious how he'd died. Internal injuries, not to mention numerous broken bones and major blood loss.

Joey took one look and immediately turned his head and threw up. I dragged the body clear of the area and laid it on the ground. There was nothing to cover it with yet, so I pulled the victim's shirt up over his face.

His seat was loose on its mounts, and with a little prodding I was able to pull it free and jerk it out of the plane. I climbed in and released the woman's seat belt. A quick check of her jugular confirmed a weak but steady pulse, but she was having difficulty taking a breath. Although I didn't know the extent of her injuries, whether she had any broken bones in her spine or anywhere else, I had to get her in a position where she could breathe. From the sound of it, something was blocking her windpipe.

The man next to her, whom I thought to be a goner, suddenly groaned and stirred. He mumbled something, the tone a plea for help but the words themselves unintelligible.

"It's okay. Help is here," I told him. "We'll get you out." But what then? I asked myself.

He struggled, still bent forward, and moaned again. "Sit still," I told him. "You'll be okay. The lady needs help worse than you." I didn't know if that was true, but it did appear her needs were more immediate. At least he could breathe.

I clutched the woman gently under her arms and pulled her toward me, as though we were preparing to embrace, all the while praying that God wouldn't let her injuries worsen at my hand. What I was doing was risky, without question, but I had to get her out of the plane and into a position where her mouth and throat could drain so she could breathe. She was choking on her own blood.

With her body now bent forward, her head drooping over my shoulder, she drained as I'd hoped, and the gurgling stopped. Her breath was shallow, but I could hear air exchange, although it was still raspy. I could tell she had lost some teeth and hoped that was the main source of the bleeding.

I backed slowly to the cabin door, keeping her close to me, her arms hanging limp, her head bobbing on my shoulder. As I eased a foot out, my toe found the ground, and I inched out until I could put my other leg down.

"Joey, give me a hand!" I called.

I heard him come over, and out of the corner of my eye I saw his ashen face, unwiped fluid glistening on his chin.

"I need to lay her down easy," I said. "Once you can get close enough, grab her legs and we'll lay her on her back. Don't jostle her too much. We don't know how badly injured she is."

"How about him?" Joey said haltingly, moving a thumb toward the man in the plane.

"He's in shock but conscious," I told him. "Probably doesn't know what's going on." I'd seen it before — a guy with his legs cut off by a train, swearing at us and telling us to pull up his pants. "You ready? Okay — one, two, three, lift. That's it. Now back over here, right, good. Okay, set her down nice and easy."

Joey put her legs down and helped me lay her gently on her back. When I let go of her, he helped me stand. Though still unconscious, she was breathing better. But I feared lying on her back would fill her airway with fluid again.

"We need to roll her onto her side," I told Joey, "so her throat can drain. She's got some teeth knocked out, but it might be worse than it looks. With all that bleeding she might not be able to breathe on her back like this too long."

I spied the luggage bay door on the fuselage, told Joey to hold on, and trotted over to it. Inside was baggage but also some emergency equipment — blankets, flares, an ice chest. I grabbed a couple of blankets and returned to the woman.

Folding a blanket, I directed Joey into position. We rolled her gently onto her side and put the blanket behind her, easing her back onto it. She stayed on her side, and I watched as more fluid drained from her mouth. I covered her with the other blanket, wishing I had laid her on top of one also. But there weren't enough. The storage compartment only held three.

"What about him?" Joey asked, nodding toward the plane.

"I'd say his legs are broken pretty good, and I think he's pinned, but he seems okay otherwise. I can't really tell. He's semiconscious, and that's a good sign. Lots of pain, I'm sure, but I think he'll be better off if we don't move him." I stood and surveyed my surroundings, realizing for the first time what a predicament we were in.

"Joey," I said solemnly, "you have to go for help."

"Huh?"

"We don't even know if someone's missed

these people yet, or if they were able to radio in their problem or location. There might be a search and rescue chopper on the way, and there might not."

I thought a second. "Look, you go back down the cliff — you can rappel, can't you?"

"Of course." He scowled and finally wiped the back of his hand across his chin.

"Okay. You shinny on down to the cabin and have Mr. Curran and Lt. Brown drive you into town. Notify the sheriff, and tell them we have two injured people up here — one serious, the other life-threatened — and two deceased. Tell them they'll need a helicopter that can carry two on gurneys. Or two choppers. Or they'll have to make two trips." I glanced up. It was a couple hours after noon, I figured. "You'd better hurry. They'll need daylight. Otherwise we're stuck here all night. I'll make a fire so they can find us."

Joey hesitated, looking from me to the woman to the dead man, still uncovered on the ground nearby.

"Hurry!" I shouted as I bent over the woman. Joey ran off without a word, and I prayed he'd make it okay. I was confident he would. God had gotten us this far. Rappeling without a belay was risky, but it was the only hope we had. I had no idea how long it would take — or even if it was possible — to hike into town without going down the cliff. For all I knew, the other directions all led deeper into the wilderness.

When I was sure the woman was okay, for a few minutes at least, I returned to the plane, pulling the pilot out and dragging him over next to the other dead man. I glanced unconsciously at the face of the first one — the kind of glance where you know what you are going to see, know it isn't a pretty sight, but are drawn to look anyway — and a flicker of recognition sent a chill up my spine.

Turning my head toward the plane slowly, almost hesitantly, I took a closer look at the badly damaged tail and realized this was the plane we'd seen earlier at the airport, the one with the marking on the tail that matched the emblem on the door of the Land Rover.

I stared at the marking, recognizing the oriental-styled black H on a red circle — a rising sun.

Moving to the fuselage, I leaned in and spoke to the groaning man, his pained face now turned toward me, his narrow eyes pleading.

I spoke softly and firmly, hoping to inspire confidence. "Help is on the way, Hiromoto-san."

SIX

For just a moment — that brief passage of time we tend to liken to a split second when we're fifty yards from the goal with ten seconds to play and we're behind by five points, and to an eternity when we're in front of an audience and we've forgotten what we were going to say — for that span of time I sat down on the floor of the airplane with my feet outside on the ground and just listened. A slight breeze had picked up and rustled the trees, birds once again returned to their normal habits, squirrels raced past me and darted up tree trunks.

I enjoyed the clear blue sky and the light of the sun on the tops of the trees that stretched high enough above their neighbors to catch its waning yellow rays. It looked like another beautiful sunset was in order.

Too bad I wouldn't enjoy it. With a sigh, I pushed my aching body up and went back to work. Some vacation.

I had to build a fire, a nice big one so they could find us quickly. Joey could direct them, sure, but I was hoping they were already looking for us. And I had to plan for the unlikely possibility that Joey wouldn't make it. Hey, bad things happen.

I had three people to keep warm and at least two to feed if I could. I didn't know if the woman would be able to eat, even if she was conscious. I looked around for the bag of food I'd been carrying all morning, then remembered to my disappointment that it was at the bottom of the cliff. It might as well have been in my refrigerator at home.

First things first. I checked my patients once more, just to make sure they were still with me. Mr. Hiromoto was complaining about being hungry and thirsty and in pain. Well, he wasn't exactly complaining. He nodded in the affirmative when I asked about those things. Otherwise, he didn't say much.

The woman looked familiar, although it was hard to be sure with the damage to her face. She was definitely Japanese, but I could tell nothing beyond that. I didn't ask Hiromoto about her. It really didn't make any difference at this point. The dead man — not the pilot, but the first man I'd pulled free of the plane — was Mr. Wakigama, Hiromoto's interpreter. I'd miss him. He was a nice guy.

I trekked through the trees, picking up as many dry branches as I could carry, returning with armload after armload. This blaze would have to double as a signal fire and something to keep us warm all night. Even now, in the late afternoon, I noticed a drop in the temperature.

I found an emergency kit in the plane's luggage compartment, then built a large mound of kindling and tossed in a flare. There was a loud whoosh as the fuel ignited. I tossed some more wood onto the tall, hot fire and returned to the plane.

I assumed they'd already been fishing, just as Michelle had suggested. I saw some Polaroid photos on the floor of the plane, and while Hiromoto napped, I took a peek. They were of him and the other members of his group at Manzanar. I recognized the stone guard houses and the cemetery obelisk. Their faces were solemn, without a smile among them except on a girl, and hers was subdued, almost embarrassed. She had nice teeth.

There was an ice chest in the luggage compartment, so I dragged it out and opened it. Fog from dry ice wafted out, which to my mind could only mean one thing — frozen fish.

Sure enough, several whole trout stared up at me through Ziploc bags. The fish weren't completely stiff, and I hoped they'd been gutted. Careful not to touch the dry ice, I shifted the load and saw a bottle of water.

Back in the luggage compartment I found another blanket. This I spread over Hiromoto, who was still asleep. His breathing was regular, though shallow, and his pulse was okay. I took a closer look at his legs. They were jammed behind the broken pilot seat, and sheet metal from the damaged fuselage was wrapped around — and very likely extending into — his legs, although his trousers hid the extent of the damage. There was not a lot of blood or any obvious deformities, but I feared that in trying to release the seat and extricate his limbs, I might start a chain reaction I was ill-equipped to handle.

Hiromoto stirred and groaned. "Where am I?" he asked in perfect English.

"It's okay, sir," I told him. "You've been in a plane crash, remember?"

He looked around, then shut his eyes. "Ah, it is so. I had hoped . . ." He trailed off, but I assumed he meant that he wished it was a dream. Then reality struck him, and he gaped at the empty seat beside him. Tears filled his eyes instantly.

"The girl?" I asked. "She's outside, lying down. She'll be okay, I think."

"Then she's not dead?"

"No, sir. She's injured, I'll not lie to you about that, but I don't think it's life-threatening. I've made her as comfortable as I can."

"Thank you. Can you get me out so I can see her?" he asked.

I scooted to the backseat and sat next to him. "Hiromoto-san, I don't believe we should try. I can't do anything for you if you start to bleed, nor can I protect your legs if they are broken. And if you have any other injuries, they might be made worse by moving you. Help is on the way. In the meantime, you're going to have to stay put."

For the first time he looked directly at me. "Ah, yes, you know my name. You said it before, but I didn't fully realize . . . Do I know you? You seem familiar to me."

"Gil Beckman, sir. We met at the park. I was the one who —"

"Saved my life!" he exclaimed. "Yes, it is you. And now you again save my life. How is it this happens?"

"Luck or coincidence, some would say," I told him. "But I believe God had His hand in it. The important thing is, I'm here, and you're going to be okay as soon as we can get you out of here."

"How did you come to be here in this forest?"

117

"I came up here on vacation to go fishing. A friend of mine wanted to do some rock climbing, so I came along to help him. We saw your plane go down while we were climbing."

"Where is this friend? I need to —" A crease of pain rippled briefly across his face. "I need to thank him as well."

"He's gone back for help. Left a couple hours ago. Should be in town by now." *I hope.* I looked over my shoulder at the darkening sky and knew help wouldn't be coming until morning. I spread the remaining blanket over Hiromoto, and he nodded. I was dying to ask what had been done to his grandson, but I knew enough about their culture to realize it was none of my business. Eric Hiromoto had plotted against his grandfather to take over the company — by means of his grandfather's death. But we had no proof that would stand up in court, so we were forced to let him go and let Hiromoto deal with him as he saw fit.

"I'll check on you later," I told him. "Let me check on the young lady, then I'll fix some dinner, okay?" I backed out of the fuselage without waiting for a response and knelt by the girl. To my surprise, her eyes were open, and she stared at me, not really afraid, just confused.

"Oh, hello," I said softly. "It's okay. Don't try to talk. My name's Gil. You were in a plane crash, remember?"

She nodded slightly.

"Okay, good. That you remember, I mean. I think you're going to be okay. Help is on the way. It's dark now, so we'll have to wait until morning." I smiled. She wanted to smile back, I'm sure of it, but somehow she knew she couldn't. Maybe the pain, the swelling, maybe her tongue had explored her mouth and she knew she'd been hurt there. Instead, she began to cry silently, great tears welling up in her black eyes and spilling onto her cheeks and dropping onto the ground.

I brushed my thumb on my pants, then gently wiped the stains off her cheeks and the bridge of her nose.

She'd be the age of my daughter if I had one, I thought and was surprised by it. It was an odd idea, and I wondered what made me think of it.

"Listen, I don't know your name, honey," I said in my most fatherly voice. "You can't speak, so how about if I call you Mary for now? Is that okay?" I couldn't call her Hey You or Honey all night long. I never thought to ask Hiromoto.

She blinked once.

"Okay, one blink for yes, two for no. Is

that what you're telling me?"

She blinked once. I smiled. That was good. We were making progress. "Are you warm enough?" She blinked once but strained her eyes toward the ground. "You don't like the dirt and leaves and stuff, is that it? All right, I'll find you something. Be right back."

I jumped up, threw some wood on the fire, and trudged back to the plane. In the rear of the luggage compartment was a suitcase. It was locked, but a few seconds with a large rock and it opened. Obviously not a Samsonite. I rifled through it, noticing the men's clothing inside was too large for Hiromoto. Must be the pilot's stuff. I grabbed a couple sweatshirts, one for her head and one for me to wear, and a couple pair of pants to spread under her. For the first time I noticed the chill, and with the sun completely gone, I knew it would get much colder before long.

I dropped everything beside her as she watched my every move. I gazed at the blanket keeping her propped on her side. I figured I'd need that blanket, so I looked for something to replace it with. The passenger seat I'd pulled out and discarded caught my eye. It was broken and nearly straight. I retrieved it and set it gently behind her, removing the blanket.

"That okay?" I asked. She nodded, and I went to work putting the trousers underneath her, rolling her back and forth until, inch by inch, I was able to work them into place. Then I put the sweatshirt over her and replaced her blanket. When I was done, she visibly relaxed. It had been a difficult few minutes.

With my patients in relative comfort, I pulled everything out of the plane to see what I could use. There was a thermos full of cold coffee on the cockpit floor, and I found a piece of polished aluminum from somewhere on the plane, about the size and shape of a hubcap, to heat it in. First I tossed the piece in the fire to sterilize it, then wiped it out with a pair of jammies from the pilot's suitcase, poured in the coffee, and set it by the edge of the fire, over some hot coals. It took a while to heat, but when it was drinkable I poured it back into the thermos and shared it with Mr. Hiromoto. He took the thermos cap in silence, dipping his head toward me out of gratitude and respect, then drank it quickly.

"You want some fish?" I asked. "You need to eat something."

He nodded. "Yes, please."

"Okay. Coming up, sir."

Using a pair of socks for protection, I moved the dry ice and took out the bag of fish. I placed them on the aluminum dish and stuck them over the fire, turning them as best I could with a fingernail file from the pilot's personal hygiene kit, after I'd sterilized it in the fire, of course.

The business tycoon ate heartily, thanking me again profusely. He never again complained about his injuries or his predicament, but the pain was evident on his face.

Mary watched me from her makeshift bed by the fire, her eyes speaking of her hunger and apprehension. I showed her the fish.

"Would you like to try?" I asked. "If I give you small amounts, you won't have to chew, just swallow."

She nodded pitifully and opened her mouth. I forced myself not to wince at the bloody gap where her teeth had been. I shoveled a small amount into her mouth and dropped it on the back of her tongue, and she swallowed with her eyes shut. They watered but didn't cry. She prepared for another bite.

Five or six bites were all she could take, but I was greatly encouraged. Oh, she could have gone all night without food and wouldn't be any the worse for it. But I took it as a sign that she would be okay, or at

122

least that she wasn't getting worse. I searched the ice chest and found the bottle of mountain spring water in the bottom. It wasn't too cold, so I unscrewed the cap and poured a little into her mouth without making contact with her lips — to prevent contamination — and she took it with obvious relief.

"Now rinse your mouth out, then spit," I suggested, holding an empty Ziploc bag under her mouth, and she did so, eliminating bloody water, then settled back. She closed her eyes, and I stepped away to leave her in peace.

Retreating to the plane, I let Mr. Hiromoto take a turn at the water bottle, then went out to toss some more logs on the fire. I settled down next to it, realizing, once I was still, how tired I was.

Soon a strange calm washed over me, and I listened to the flames snap and hiss and the movement of unseen nocturnal animals in the woods surrounding the clearing. The stars were obliterated by the light of the fire and its smoke, but I stared skyward anyway.

I remembered being a kid at summer church camp in the mountains and going out at night after a truly inspirational service and finding an isolated rock where I could sit by myself and feel spiritual and look up into the night sky at the stars. Then I asked

God to open the sky and show me a glimpse of heaven, not so I could believe but because I believed. Just a little glimpse so He could prove to me that I was special to Him.

That it didn't happen didn't shake my faith, which might indicate how strong my faith was — or how weak, that I should even ask such a ridiculous thing and actually expect God to answer. I waited and prayed and waited, then shrugged my young shoulders and hiked back to the cabin to short-sheet someone's bunk and put soap on their toothbrush.

I awakened some time later — how much time had elapsed I wasn't sure, nor did I know what had brought me out of my sleep. Stretching my neck to relieve a cramped muscle, I shivered in my shirt sleeves and then stoked the fire anew, adding wood to the hot coals, which erupted into new flames immediately.

Turning to check Mary, I saw she was watching me.

"How are you doing, sweetheart?" I asked. "Warm enough?"

She shook her head.

"Me neither," I admitted. "You want some water or anything?"

No, she said with her head.

"I've built the fire up. You should warm

up pretty soon. What's the matter? Boy, I wish you could talk."

"I can," she said in a hoarse whisper, barely audible above the crackling blaze.

I moved closer and lay down on the bare ground with my face near hers, so I could hear her without making her strain.

"Thank you," she said.

"For what?" I asked.

"Taking care of uth." She lisped because of the missing teeth.

"No problem," I assured her. "I'm glad I was here."

"Am I really methed up?"

I shook my head. "No. You lost a couple teeth, as I'm sure you've already figured out. Otherwise, you're still as pretty as a picture. A few bruises maybe, but they'll fade in time. What's your name?"

She smiled — a little one, but a smile nonetheless. "Mary."

"No way! You're putting me on."

"Yeth. It'th Hiromi."

"Hiromi. That's very pretty. Hiromi Hiromoto?"

She shook her head slowly. "He'th my great-uncle, my grandmother'th brother. But I'm named after him."

"That's interesting. I'm Gil. Named after a fish."

She suppressed a giggle. "I know. You told me."

"Oh, yeah, I guess I did." I stared at her eyes for a moment, pretty black eyes in which I could see the reflection of the flames behind me. "You know, you look a little familiar to me. Have we met?" Under any other circumstances, that might be mistaken for a pick-up line, but not here, not now. Truth is, she did look familiar. It's just that it was a little hard to tell with all that facial trauma.

"At the offith," she said. "Eric."

I snapped my fingers. "That's right! Eric Hiromoto's receptionist. You brought me tea and cookies."

"Coffee," she corrected. "And Englith thortbread."

I smiled. "Good memory. So, do you re-member what happened?"

She shook her head.

"You don't remember the crash, or you don't remember anything?"

"The crath." A distressed look crossed her face.

"Okay, don't worry about it," I told her. "I'm sorry I asked. You need to rest, okay? We'll talk later if you want — it's up to you."

"Pleathe thtay," she whimpered. "I'm afraid."

"I don't blame you," I admitted. She reached out shakily with a hand encrusted with dried blood and took one of mine. Her skin was like ice, and my heart went out to her. I held her hand and brushed her face lightly to give her comfort, and she closed her eyes. When she finally drifted back to sleep I cried for her — and for myself, I suppose. I saw in her the daughter I never had, and the high school girl who would marry me, then die unexpectedly . . . Would we actually get out of here? Would help come in the morning? I hadn't thought about it until that moment, but . . . had God led me up here so I could perish with these people?

I didn't think so. I settled myself down with a prayer for Hiromi, for myself, for Hiromoto, for the families of the dead men, and most certainly for Joey.

If he didn't make it back for help and I died out here, I'd kill him, that's what I'd do.

No, I knew he'd make it. I trusted God for that. He put us here for this, of that I had no doubt. What men might call coincidence, I called providence. God's planning. He gave me skills to use, then positioned me to make the best use of them. Joey, too. That I should be this far from home and be in the right place to help someone I knew who was also far from home — only God could orchestrate something like that. In that sense it was a partnership, and part of the reason Paul the apostle cautioned us to be content regardless of our circumstances. We are in them because God wants us in them and has a purpose for us in them.

Coincidence? From the perspective of carnal man, perhaps. From the viewpoint of the Christian, no way.

A moan from the plane interrupted my discourse. I carefully peeled Hiromi's hand from mine, set it down easily, and walked quietly to the crumpled fuselage. Hiromoto writhed and moaned in his prison, his eyes closed but sleep eluding him, and he shivered uncontrollably. He was too far from the fire and not getting enough heat.

I retrieved the remaining blanket, the one I had been using, and covered him with it, then took the rest of the clothes from the pilot's suitcase and spread them over him. His eyes opened, and I could see the appreciation in them.

"You should warm up pretty good now, Hiromoto-san. I'll build a small fire close by, upwind. I wish I could do more for you."

"You . . . do much," he said, then turned his head away from me to hide his pain.

128

I gathered some kindling and a few logs and built a mound a few feet from the plane. I lit a flare and tossed it in, and soon a smaller but definitely hot fire was blazing, reflecting off his pale face. In a few minutes he had stopped shivering.

I returned to the main fire, stoked it, and got as close as I could. Curling up in a ball, I let my fatigue take me, hoping I could fall asleep before I got too cold.

I don't remember falling asleep. I lay there, seeing the forest around me, and began to hear a strange sound. There was gunfire around me, and shouts, and the strange sound grew louder and closer. It was a regular, repetitive noise, kind of a *whop whop whop*. Then it was deafening, yet I didn't care. I ran toward it, then saw the dark helicopter rise above the trees, and I broke for the open door, where a man in a green uniform sat, raining machine gun fire around me at the enemy. I sloshed through the rice paddy, my shoes threatening to stick in the thick mud. I was almost to the chopper when an explosion to my right sent water and debris screaming toward me —

Suddenly I sat up in a cold sweat, my heart pounding. I gazed around me in a panic, searching for a clue as to where I was. The helicopter was still descending, but it was white, with no machine gunner in the door. It was descending into my clearing, full of rescuers. I breathed easier, relieved that the horror of Vietnam wasn't real.

An odd dream in the first place, considering I'd never been to Vietnam.

I jumped up and began waving as the chopper settled to the ground, the whipping blades raising swirls of dirt and smoke from my dying fire. The door opened, and Joey leaped out with a shout as Hiromoto cried out from inside the mangled airplane.

Rescue workers piled out and raced over to us. Two medics went to work on Hiromi while another chopper arrived and landed and more folks exited to assist, including a man dressed in a khaki shirt, forest green trousers, and a gold star on his left breast.

As they assessed Hiromoto's situation, Joey came over to me and we hugged, a little awkwardly at first, but we both seemed to settle into it.

Hiromoto moaned as the side of the airplane was cut away from his leg. They wrapped the wounds and splinted both legs, then lifted him out and placed him on a litter. Hiromi had already been carried to a chopper, and Hiromoto followed. A medic trotted over to me, but I waved him off.

"Get them out of here," I ordered. He waved and retreated, and the choppers took off with their patients, in and out in less than ten minutes.

The sheriff moseyed over to Joey and me as the helicopters cleared the treetops.

"They'll be back for us and the deceased in a bit," he explained. He reached out to shake my hand. "I'm Ben Thomas, sheriff of this county. I owe both of you a great big thanks. This was a right good thing you did. Real handy, you being where you were."

"God's doing, I'm sure," I said.

"I believe that," he assented. "I surely do. Joey here tells me you used to be a cop."

"He ought to know," I muttered.

"Good thing, I say. You knew what to do."

"Well, I can't rightly say driving a patrol car downtown, wrestling drunks, separating feuding spouses, and poking around people's insides at autopsies exactly prepared me for climbing, doctoring, and building signal fires."

"Thinking on your feet, son. That's what I'm talking about. Being ready for anything, always prepared."

"Sounds like a Boy Scout," Joey said.

"Nothing wrong with that," Sheriff Thomas responded. "Boy Scouts are a good group,

131

and will continue to be unless they let the ACLU infiltrate it with gays and atheists."

"Hear, hear," I echoed.

"Say, you wouldn't be looking for a job, now, would you?"

"Well, not exactly . . ." This was so sudden, so unexpected, I didn't know what to say. I supposed working up here would be neat, but I hadn't given it much thought. It's too easy to stay where one is comfortable — or familiar, at least — even if it's not what one really wants. The job I had might be terrible, but at least it was a known quantity. Kind of.

"I'll give it some thought," I said. The idea of leaving Sally didn't really sound like something I wanted to do. Would she come with me? Leave everything — her job, her home, her friends — to follow me to some out-of-the-way place where the word *mall* (when spoken anyway) means something that happens to you in the woods when you meet an angry bear?

Nah, it'd never happen.

"I'll think about it," I repeated. "But I doubt it. I have a good job. Thanks for asking though."

"Okay," he said. He pulled something out of the pocket of his khaki shirt and stuck it out toward me. "Gum?"

"No thanks." I sat down on a fallen tree.

"I'll have some," Joey said quickly. The sheriff gave him a piece, then took one for himself, adding it to the wad he was already chewing.

"Shouldn't be too long now," he said to no one in particular as he surveyed the damaged plane, his hands in his pockets.

"What about the FAA and the NTSB?" I asked. "They en route?"

"They'll start wandering in this afternoon. I'll let them know where you're staying. They'll probably want to talk to you two, seeing as how you witnessed it. Got any ideas what happened?"

I shook my head. "Not a clue. Engine trouble, it sounded like, but beyond that I don't know. The survivors didn't know anything. Maybe they'll remember something later."

"Hmmm." He nodded, and we all fell silent, one of those uncomfortable natural pauses when everyone runs out of things to say at the same time. I took it upon myself to break it.

"You leave the rope tied up at the top of the cliff?" I asked Joey.

"Yeah, why?"

"I thought I'd rappel down."

"You sure?"

"Hey, down is easy. I used to be on the SWAT team, remember?"

"You don't want a ride down in the chopper?" Sheriff Thomas wondered. "You look awful tired."

"Thanks for your concern, both of you," I said. "But helicopters and I don't get along too well."

"I'll go with you," Joey volunteered.

"Someone has to untie the rope when I'm down," I reminded him. "And haul the bags back."

"I'll do it," the sheriff said. "You guys deserve a little fun. I'll bring them by your cabin later."

I shrugged. "Okay by me." I pushed myself up with a grunt. "Let's go then. No sense waiting around here any longer. Sheriff, I'll see you later. Thanks for showing up. Good thing you had access to the choppers."

"That's the way it is up here. We all help each other out."

At the top of the cliff I strapped on the nylon harness and attached a figure eight to the carabiner I'd threaded onto the D-ring. I hooked on the rope and backed to the edge of the cliff, tugging on the leather, fingerless gloves. With my left hand holding the rope behind me — to act as a brake when I moved my arm to a more extreme position — and my right hand encircling the rope in the front, I nodded at Joey.

"When I'm down I'll tie the harness on, and you can haul it back up. What are you going to do about your chocks?"

"No problem, I can haul them up from here. They should break loose. The ones that don't, I'll get on the way down."

"See you at the bottom then. Later, Sheriff."

He touched the brim of his hat.

I stepped back slowly, off the edge of the rock, and walked backwards down the face of the cliff, letting the rope slip slowly through my right hand while I tested the braking with my left. It had been a few years since I'd rappelled — standard training for SWAT — and it took a few feet to get my sea legs.

Once I was comfortable, I bent my knees, sprang backward, and let the rope slide freely through my right hand. The top of the cliff receded quickly. As the pendulum effect of the rope brought me back toward the cliff, I moved my left arm and slowed my descent as I bent my legs to prepare for my first landing.

A helicopter approached from the west, and I watched it as I hung on the mountain. I wasn't afraid of heights, really. But I was

135

afraid of the sudden stops that always came at the bottom. Hanging from the rapelling rope didn't bother me. It was something I had done many times, was comfortable with, and for the most part took no effort. Free climbing, with no ropes and no safety devices — that was pure insanity. I couldn't imagine ever doing that. That and climbing down from the top of a roller coaster. I'd had enough of that for a lifetime, thank you.

A rocking chair by the fire, that was my speed.

But since I was here, I might as well enjoy it.

"You okay?" a voice from above shouted down. It was Joey, wondering why I'd stopped.

"Just enjoying the view," I shouted. He waved, and the roped we'd climbed up with, still attached to the camming devices and chocks, began jerking its way up the rock face as Joey pulled it from above.

I took in the mountains and forests and our fishing lake, part of which I could see from here. I was at peace, hanging there, and it was truly a spiritual moment. I sighed and thanked God out loud for the wonder and beauty of His creation, then sprang away from the cliff.

SEVEN

The hike home had been good, and Joey even asked me some questions about God and Christianity. Nothing too deep, mind you, but it was tremendous progress when you consider what he'd been like just a year before. He was softening, and I trusted that God would bring him soon to the point where he would be able to understand sin and his need for a Savior. Then and only then would I be able to reach him with the Gospel. One thing was sure — our adventure had broken down whatever was left of the wall between us.

Rounding the last bend in the trail before the cabin, I saw the rear fender of a green Jeep parked on the near side of our hideaway, partially obscured by the trees. I suspected it was the sheriff, and as more of the vehicle came into view my assumption proved correct. It was the same Jeep I had seen in front of the office when we first rolled into town.

He'd brought Joey's equipment by. The smoke curled out of the chimney, and I figured he'd taken a seat and decided to stay a while. He was that kind of guy, the local neighborhood sheriff everybody knows and likes. Everyone's good buddy.

We trudged the final yards to the door and went in, finding Theo, Hal, and Sheriff Thomas sitting around the fireplace drinking coffee and munching on cookies, cookies I didn't know we'd had. Hal caught me staring at the package.

"Sheriff Thomas brought them, Gil. We weren't holding out on you."

I smiled the smile of the guilty and extended my hand to the sheriff. "Good to see you again."

He took it warmly as he stood. "Guess I beat you down."

"It's a longer walk than I remembered, and you had a helicopter and a Jeep, if I'm not mistaken."

Sheriff Thomas chuckled.

"In other words, you got lost," Theo said.

"No, we didn't. We just took our time so we could enjoy God's creation without your whining to ruin it." I grabbed a seat and a handful of cookies. I didn't need coffee right then. Oxygen, yes, coffee, no.

"Lt. Brown tells me you're looking for a job," the sheriff said, getting right to the point. "Like I said, we could use a man of your experience up here."

I gave Theo a vacant glance, then said to

138

the sheriff, "I appreciate that, but like *I* said, I have a job."

"Security guard," he said, nodding. His tone wasn't derogatory, but the way he looked at me and the way he didn't say anything else told me what he thought about my position. Then again, I pretty much thought the same thing.

"I enjoy it," I said, "and frankly, it's been a lot of fun the past year or so."

"So I read."

"Read?"

"Yeah. All the disasters down there made the news. People dying right and left in an amusement park — that makes for pretty good reading."

"Disaster Park," Joey said.

"Come on," I said to the sheriff, "not that many people died."

"Well, it seemed like a lot. Anyway, the stories said Lt. Brown solved them all with the help of an unnamed park security guard."

Theo laughed, and Harold moaned. Joey got a kick out of it too but didn't say anything — wisely so.

"That's about it," I conceded. To Theo I commented, "Bet I know who wrote the press releases." He just shrugged and grinned.

The sheriff continued, "But Lt. Brown filled me in on what really happened. And I thought, since you can't go back to the P.D. down there, why don't you come up here? You can't argue about the quality of life. We have it all — fishing, boating, skiing, hiking, perfect weather, peace —"

"Plane crashes, murder," I said.

He nodded. "I guess you have that wherever you have people. You read about our little homicide then?"

Hal said, "Murder? What's that all about?"

"It was in the paper the other day," the sheriff said. "A local real estate agent — a female — was found dead in her car. Blunt force trauma to the head. Looks like she was molested too. Say, I wonder if you guys —" He looked from me to Theo. "— wouldn't mind helping me. With your combined homicide experience, you might be able to dig up a couple clues for me."

"Busman's holiday," Hal observed.

"What's a busman's holiday?" Joey asked.

"That's the vacation they get as a reward for being promoted from busboy to busman," I explained.

"Huh?"

"Don't listen to him," Theo said. "It's when the guy who drives a cross-country bus

140

goes on vacation and drives a family or friends around on a cross-country bus. It refers to anyone who does on vacation what they do at work."

"Anyway," I said, "I don't see what we could find that your people haven't already uncovered."

"They're all pretty new," he said. "I'm retired L.A.P.D. but I never worked homicide. Rode a motorcycle my whole career. Came up here to live the good life, but after seeing what a mess the previous sheriff made of the department — he was a civilian, ran a tackle shop — I decided to run for sheriff. And here I am."

He rose from his chair. "Nonetheless, you're right. I didn't mean to impose. You're here to have fun, relax, catch some fish. Anyway, you've already done enough," he added, looking at me. "That's really what I hung around for, to thank you again." He grabbed his Smokey Bear hat from the moose antlers over the fireplace. "Thanks. You did a great job. Those people owe you their lives." He reached out to shake my hand again.

"Thank you for saying so," I said in uncharacteristic humility.

He stuck his hat on his balding head. "Well, enjoy yourselves. And watch out for the killer." He winked. Joey's face blanched. Hal's eyebrows raised. Theo and I looked at each other and rolled our eyes.

We followed him outside and watched him drive off, waving to us out of the open car window just before he disappeared into the trees.

"So, what do you think?" I asked Theo.

"About what?"

"About helping him with the murder."

"I don't know, what do you think?"

"You know what I think."

"I'll think about it. Right now I'm thinking about dinner."

"Me too."

We turned and went back inside the cabin. To think.

The morning dawned bright, clear, and early. Our rising was staggered — Hal, me, Theo, and Joey, in that order. Hal stoked the fire and made coffee, and by the time Joey had dragged his young carcass out of the sack, the rest of us were enjoying pan biscuits and bacon and eggs.

Hal wanted to fish, but Joey wasn't interested. Theo had some reading he wanted to catch up on. And I was too tired and sore from my climb to go out, at least this early. I wouldn't admit that, of course, not in front of Joey. Theo and Hal knew good and well I was paying for my crime. I told them I thought I'd take it easy for a day, then go out the next to give fishing another try. That would be the last day of our trip, and I wouldn't have another chance for a while, but I just couldn't motivate myself to get out there right then.

Undaunted, Hal grabbed his gear and lit out, and in a few minutes we heard the small outboard sputter to life. I played some solitaire, fiddled around with the fire, and watched Joey put away his climbing gear, but I couldn't get over the restless feeling I had. It was tough — feeling restless but unable to do anything.

Hal came back in a couple hours, empty-handed. I didn't feel so bad then. We had lunch — some canned chili poured over fried Spam slices with chocolate donuts on the side — then returned to our pre-banquet activities. A half-hour hadn't passed before Hal couldn't take it any longer. I guess our restlessness showed.

"Would you guys go into town . . . please?"

"Why?" Theo asked.

"You're driving me crazy."

"We're not doing anything," I protested.

"That's the point," Hal said. "You two

know you want to be helping that sheriff. And, Joey, you want to go talk to that little clerk at the market, am I right?"

We looked at each other.

"Well . . ." I began.

"Take my truck," Hal said, tossing the keys into the air.

I jumped up and snagged them. "I'm driving!" I shouted, and we all scrambled out the door. My aches and pains had miraculously dissipated, and new life had been bestowed upon us all.

We dropped Joey off at the market, with last-minute warnings regarding his future ability to walk should he step off the straight and narrow, and told him to meet us at the sheriff's station in two hours — or less. But I figured even if she told him to take a long walk on a short plank, he'd find something to keep himself busy. I'd noticed a movie theater nearby, with a couple of recent movies playing, action-adventure flicks he'd probably like, and one of those Dumb Teenager movies he'd probably think was an intellectual excursion.

I parked outside, and we walked into the lobby. The sheriff's Jeep was outside, so we figured he'd be there. But the dispatcher/receptionist/records clerk/building code enforcement officer who greeted us — quite warmly, I might add — said he was at dinner.

"He eats early," she explained, even though we hadn't asked.

"When do you expect him back?" I asked.

"I don't know. Not too long, I wouldn't think. Are you the cops from down the hill?"

"Our fame has preceded us," I remarked.

"Sheriff Thomas said to have you come on in when — that is, *if* you showed up. He left the stuff out on the table in his office. Come on through." She buzzed the door, Theo pushed it open, and soon she was leading us down a short hall into a small office filled with bookcases and a desk and a round table upon which were several manila folders. She nodded toward them and shut the door as she retreated.

"He apparently had us pegged," I observed wryly. Theo grunted and opened one of the folders casually, trying not to act very interested, while I scanned the room. The walls were adorned with the usual photos and certificates, most of the former of a younger Sheriff Thomas in L.A.P.D. blues grinning from the back of a Harley or Kawasaki. In a couple of them Thomas and some other motor cops rode in formation, standing on their heads or completing other intricate feats of two-wheeled magic. I recognized Pasadena on January 1st in one of the photos.

"Well?" I asked, turning back to Theo. He had pulled up a chair and was going through the reports in greater detail.

"Sit down," he ordered. "You check out the evidence, I'll read the factual report, then we'll switch."

I obeyed and took out a handful of color photos, thumbing through them slowly.

"Pretty gruesome," I noted. She had apparently been found in the trunk of her car, dead before she was put there from the looks of it. She'd been dismembered. She'd been wearing a jogging suit and tennis shoes.

The surrounding area had also been photographed but didn't show much besides pretty scenery. There were no houses visible in any of the photos, but that didn't mean there weren't any. The trees were pretty thick in the area. I take it back — the scenery wasn't pretty . . . it was magnificent. If you had to be bludgeoned to death and stuffed in your trunk, this was the place to do it. I said as much to Theo.

"You're sick, you know that, Gil?"

"Humor keeps everything in perspective. It's an outlet."

"Here, outlet this." He handed me the

evidence report and a manila envelope. Inside were small plastic Ziploc bags containing the evidence.

There wasn't much. No fingerprints except the victim's on the car. It was a pretty safe bet the killer wore gloves. Since the victim's prints were still there, the murderer obviously hadn't just wiped the car off. Since gardening gloves or leather gloves were likely to leave their own distinctive pattern somewhere, the suspect must've worn some latex or kitchen-type gloves.

There were four items of evidence in the Ziploc bags. Trace evidence, as it is called — a few white hairs, a leaf, some fibers, and minuscule fragments of something too small to be measurable. They were almost too small to make out without a magnifying glass or a microscope, according to the report, but it said they reflected light and appeared to be multicolored. I dug into the evidence report to find out more. The hairs were found on the legs of the woman's jogging pants, the fibers and little specks in the tread of her shoes, the leaf on the floor of the trunk.

I tossed the report down on the table and gazed at Theo.

"Well?" I wondered aloud. "What do you make of it?"

"You first."

"No, if I go first you'll just say you think the same thing even if you didn't. You go first."

"And what's to stop you from doing that?"

"I don't lie."

"No more than I do. We'll take turns. What about the hairs?"

"Animal. Probably dog."

"Okay. Animal. I agree with that."

"See? You're doing it already."

"Oh, shut up, Gil. How do you know it's not a cat or some other animal?"

"They're too small to be from a polar bear."

"Okay, let's say it's from a small animal. Dog or cat?"

"A dog."

"You're positive."

"Yep."

"I've got to hear this. What makes you so sure?"

"Obviously the victim was around an animal sometime before, or at the time of, her death. Since there was no mention of similar hairs in her car or in her home and no mention that she owned a dog, let's assume they actually checked it out and all those were negative."

"They did. It's in the report you haven't read. This one." Theo held up the report he hadn't given me yet.

"That's not fair. You're not giving me access to all the information."

"You're doing fine. Remember, you're just a security guard. Besides, you could out-investigate me with one arm tied behind your back. You said so yourself."

"When?"

"Several years ago when we were getting on each other's nerves."

"Oh, yeah. I'd forgotten." I shrugged. "You're right. Sorry. Anyway, the reason I know it's a dog is because there are so few hairs, and the location. If the animal had jumped up in her lap, there'd be hairs there. There weren't. Now a cat might rub her legs, but that would leave more hairs. I don't think she let the dog get close enough to her to leave a lot of hairs, but it was running around, and just a few hairs floating about the area stuck to her. Cats aren't active enough to leave fur flying like that. Besides, they *look* like dog hairs. They're coarse. Cat hairs are finer. I'll bet she jogged by, and the dog chased her."

"Or just barked and attracted the killer's attention."

"Might have been a fenced front yard then. So you agree, those are dog hairs."

"Of course," Theo said. "The lab report

says they're dog hairs. Don't give me that look. I have the lab report here too. What about the fibers?"

"So this is a test, is it?"

"Just trying to see if you've still got it."

I harumphed. "Can't be lost," I bragged.

"So, then, what about the fibers, Mr. Know-it-all?"

"They appear to be gold. Probably carpet."

"Right again."

"Naturally."

"And the leaf?"

"I'm not clairvoyant. What's it look like?"

"Philodendron."

"Then I'd say it's a philodendron. Lab report say that?"

"No," Theo admitted. "I recognized it. Michelle has one on her porch."

"A porch plant? Then there had to be something more to it than just a jog-by. She was real estate, right?" Theo nodded. "How about this? She was jogging, saw a home, and thought she'd try and get a listing. Maybe it was just what a buyer wanted. So she goes to the front door, steps on the leaf, the guy lets her in, she steps on the carpet, the dog comes in and jumps on her, she gets murdered and raped, or raped and murdered, he drags her out and stuffs her in the trunk, he drives her car off and leaves it

150

where it was found, then walks home. So it would have to be someplace fairly close. Mile or two maybe."

"If she was jogging by, why would her car be there?"

"Okay, she drove by, on her way to jogging. Or she'd jogged by earlier and went back after she got her car. Or maybe she just liked wearing sweats and tennis shoes and wasn't jogging at all."

"Okay, that all sounds reasonable."

"Well, it's as good as solved then," I concluded.

"Huh?"

"All they have to do is look for a house with a small white dog, gold carpet, and a philodendron, probably on the porch. It's a good outdoor potted plant."

"What about the colored specks?"

"When they find the house I'm talking about, they'll figure out what the specks are."

"I think the sheriff's going to be disappointed."

"Why?"

"I think he believes we're really going to help him."

"We did. We solved it."

"Everything but the guy's name and address."

"Details, details. Besides, the local boys need to do something. It would destroy their self-respect if we city boys walk in, spend five minutes looking at their paperwork, and solve the crime for them, don't you think? Let them do the legwork and find the guy whose house meets all these criteria. Come on, let's go eat. I'm starved. Isn't there a steak house nearby?"

We left the reports on the desk and a note on top of them and excused ourselves. As we were leaving the building, we met Sheriff Thomas coming in.

"Leaving already, boys?"

Theo told him our theory.

"Well, we pretty much canvassed the area, but we can do it again. Maybe one of our rookies wasn't paying real close attention. This will give us something specific to look for. There are a couple of real strange guys up in that area."

"Don't expect it to be a strange guy, Sheriff," Theo cautioned. "Not all killers come off that way at casual encounters. Look for a place that matches the clues first, then worry about the suspect. But keep on your toes, and don't let anyone go in any place by themselves."

"I'll have my deputies check into it," Thomas said. He didn't sound too optimistic though, and I can't say I blame him. Fact is, we could have been completely wrong. It was more of an educated guess than anything, but without knowing the victim and her habits, it was all we had to go on. He thanked us, got Theo's work number, and said he'd call when they found out anything, then recommended a restaurant within walking distance and disappeared inside the station.

Theo and I enjoyed one of the best steak dinners I've ever had. Then, after picking up a cheerful but tight-lipped Joey Duncan and stopping by a roadside A-frame to get him a chili dog, we drove back to the cabin.

Fishing the following day was good, although nothing to write home about. I didn't catch anything over two pounds, but the real important thing was that no one fell out of the boat. Even Joey went along, obviously bored out of his skull, and on his first cast caught what turned out to be the biggest fish of the day, a two-and-a-half pound hatchery rainbow.

I was perfectly happy though. Content even. It was a relaxing day, what with no murders to solve, no cliffs to scale, and no plane crash victims to rescue.

The drive home the next day also proved

uneventful. Passing the airport, we could see a flurry of activity, and Theo suggested we stop in, just to save the FAA or the NTSB or whoever was investigating the plane crash, from having to call me at home. We spent an hour there while I related my story and Joey his. I didn't even bother asking the feds any questions. They don't share very well.

We hit the road again and drove straight home, not even stopping for gas, what with the dual bazillion-gallon tanks Hal had on his Road Warrior pickup. I don't even remember the trip.

EIGHT

I dragged my aching carcass into my apartment and dumped everything just inside the door. I was famished but too tired to cook, dirty but too tired to shower, tired but too tired to make it into the bedroom.

Collapsing onto the sofa, I uttered a prayer of thanks that I didn't have to go to work in the morning. The next day was Sunday, and I had all afternoon to clean my gear and put it away, launder my clothes, and get ready to go back to work that night. I'd told Sally before I left on vacation that I'd pick her up Sunday morning in the BMW. I probably needed to catch a nap Sunday afternoon, but I knew I wouldn't.

On my way to the sofa I'd noticed the flashing light on the answer machine but ignored it. Whoever it was, whatever they wanted, it could wait.

I must've dropped off to sleep — big surprise — because the ringing of the phone awakened me. I lay there gazing at the clock on the wall, trying to figure out what the big hand on the 6 and the little hand on the 11 meant, and let the machine pick up.

"Maybe I'm here, maybe I'm not," my

dulcet voice told the caller. "Leave a message and your number, and perhaps I'll call you back. If you're selling something, don't hold your breath. If you're somebody I love — you know who you are, I'll call you as soon as I get the message. As always, wait for that annoying little beep."

"Gil, it's Sally again. I was hoping you'd be home by now. I called Lt. Brown, and he said they dropped you off a couple hours ago."

Her voice was strained, worried. I sat up and pushed myself off the sofa, picking up the receiver just as she was signing off.

"I'm here," I told her as I shut off the machine. "Although I'm not sure where 'here' is. I fell asleep. It's good to hear your voice."

"Oh, Gil, I'm so glad you're back. How'd it go? Anything happen?"

"Mmmm, no, not really. You sound worried. What's up?"

"I don't know what to do. Sorry about all those messages."

"That's okay, that's what the machine's for. Besides, I haven't listened to them yet. What's up?"

"It's Elizabeth — Mrs. Potter."

"What's the matter? She sick? That might explain why she wasn't in the other day."

"You didn't see her?"

"No. Her office was empty."

Sally sighed. "That's a relief. Partially, at least."

"Sally, what's going on?"

"She's missing, Gil. She disappeared."

"As in vanished — without a trace — gone — pffft?"

"Everyone says you were the last to see her."

"But I wasn't."

"She left that message for you."

"Yes, and I went to her office, but she wasn't there. I waited around for her to come back, but she didn't. Harold and Joey were waiting for me and . . . Are you okay?" I could hear her whimpering.

"Yes. I was just so scared. Some people were saying you did something to her."

"They're evil and must be destroyed."

"Don't kid around, Gil. This is serious."

"Mrs. Potter disappearing into thin air, that could be serious. People gossiping about me doesn't mean anything."

"Can I come over, Gil? I'm worried. This isn't like her."

"That's true. If there's one thing about the Dragon Lady, she's reliable."

I looked around at my disastrous apartment, then down at myself. I sure didn't feel like driving anywhere, and it would save time if I could clean up while she was on the way over.

"Yeah, sure," I told her. "Come on over. I'm dying to see you. Oh, and pick up a pizza on the way, okay? I'm feeling spiritual."

Forty-five minutes later the doorbell rang. I'd showered and shaved, put on a pot of coffee, picked up as best I could, and cranked up the fireplace. I was concerned about Mrs. Potter, sure. But Sally was the one making my heart go pitty-pat, I must confess.

I opened the door, my smile wide, and said, "Good evening, my dear, come on in —"

"I'm not allowed . . . sweetheart," said a pimply eighteen-year-old pizza delivery guy wearing a paper hat. "But thanks for asking. That'll be twelve bucks."

I fished the money out of my jeans and handed it to him.

"Sorry there's no tip, but that's all I have." I relieved him of the pizza.

"You still have your health," he said snidely as he stomped off the porch. Just as I had almost completely shut the door, I heard a familiar voice.

"Wait, Gil, it's me."

I opened up again to see Sally hurrying up the walk. She looked very becoming in her jeans and sweater, her hair flipping from side to side as she ran in that strange little way women do. I let her in, and she brushed quickly past me.

"Thank you, it's nice to be home," I said, answering the greeting she hadn't given. I shut the door and twisted the dead bolt.

Sally dropped her purse on a chair and turned back to me, her face revealing the strain she felt.

"I'm sorry, Gil." She took the pizza box from my hand and set it on the floor, then wrapped her arms around my waist. I closed my eyes and put my arms around her shoulders. "Welcome home. I missed you," she whispered. She buried her face in my chest, and I kissed the top of her head. Her hair smelled terrific. This was nice. I'd forgotten what it was like to have someone to embrace at the end of a long day. She put her face up close to mine, and I kissed her.

"I thought it'd be quicker to call for the pizza and have it brought over instead of waiting around to pick it up," she explained when we parted.

"Cheaper too."

"Pizza was your idea." She turned and

went into the kitchen. "I'm really worried. It's not just Mrs. Potter either. There's a lot going on at the park."

I picked up the pizza and followed. "There's always something going on at the park."

"No, this is different."

I set the pizza on the table and lifted the lid while Sally grabbed two clean plates from the cupboard — the last two.

"Jerry's been fired," I said hopefully, sniffing the hot meat lover's pizza with sausage, pepperoni, and ham.

"No, just the opposite. He fired Michelle."

"What?" I was incensed. She was the one really qualified person the park had. "You must be kidding."

"I wish."

"Well, that explains Mrs. Potter's disappearance. She's in orbit. How did Jerry get away with that?"

"I don't know. And Dave Whelan —"

"He fired Dave too?"

"No. He promoted Dave. Gave him Michelle's job."

"He's a nice guy," I said, "but he's not qualified." I thought about what I'd just said and added ironically, "Which makes him perfect for the position, based on what they usually look for in a manager. The more

160

unqualified you are, the higher you can go."

On any other day Sally would have said something like, "Then there's still hope for you, Gil Beckman." But not this evening. She remained stoic as she stared at the pizza.

"When did all this happen?" I asked.

"It started with Mrs. Potter's disappearance. They didn't do much about it that day, apparently thinking after fifty years she was entitled to play hooky once. They called her house, of course, but there was no answer, so they figured she just went somewhere. But when she still didn't show the next morning they filed a report. It's been five days . . ." She trailed off and bit her lip to control her emotions. I turned my head away and busied myself filling the plates. Sally went on when she was ready.

"Then on Wednesday, Michelle is fired as soon as she walks in, just like that. Dave gets promoted on Thursday, and on Friday there were several other firings, including George Ozawa, Michelle's friend."

"He's more like a godfather to her," I mused. "I wonder what it all means." We took our food and sat down on the sofa in front of the fireplace. "I don't mean to state the obvious," I said, "but . . . she's rather old, you know. Did anyone check her house? I mean, she might have died in bed. Or maybe she fell and can't get up. Sorry, this is no time for jokes, I know. But I'm serious. Maybe she's at home."

Sally shook her head sadly. "Harry went out to her house with the police on Tuesday. She wasn't there. Nothing looked out of place. At first we thought she'd left that message for you after she came in. Some people even suggested you had something to do with her being gone, since you'd gone into her office that morning."

"That's ridiculous," I said.

"I know. But people who don't like you —"

"People attribute actions to others because it's what they would do in like circumstances. The fact is, she wasn't there when I walked in, and I couldn't wait, so I left. I figured whatever it was couldn't have been that important or she'd've been there. Apparently that wasn't the case."

"Then everyone figured she must've called from home. Jerry said there were no indications she had ever arrived. The things she usually did first hadn't been done."

Sally sat back on the sofa while I finished a piece of pizza. Hers remained untouched, so I ate it as she stared into the fire. After a few moments I put my hand on hers.

"They'll find her. Maybe she just got fed

up and took a trip. She'd be upset about Michelle's firing, and she must've known ahead of time. Or maybe she has Alzheimer's disease or something. It's possible, you know."

"It doesn't come on overnight," Sally said quietly. "You know Elizabeth. She's as sharp as a tack."

I sighed. "Yeah." What could've happened? Where'd she go, and why? For that matter, what had she wanted to see me about?

"Why did that goofball fire Michelle anyway?" I asked. "Was any reason given?"

"He's been more reclusive than ever. The official word is, they're downsizing administration now that most of the construction and renovation is complete."

"But why her? Why not someone who's a complete drain on the park's economy? Someone who is a total waste of money?"

"Like Jerry Opperman?"

"No, not *like* Jerry Opperman. Jerry Opperman!"

Sally shook her head. "He did the firing, Gil. Besides, you know as well as I, he'll have that position as long as he wants it."

"Or until the owners realize what a putz he is."

"And who's going to tell them? You? Jerry

has you buried in security —"

"Jerry?"

"You know that was his doing. Michelle didn't want to — Jerry made her."

"Why didn't he just fire me?"

"He couldn't. You're a hero. Too many questions would be asked. You're too high-profile, so he made sure Michelle put you back where you came from —"

"They're sending me to South Dakota?"

Sally ignored me. "Then he got rid of Michelle."

"How do you know all this about me?" I asked, leaning back and raising a wary eyebrow Spock-like.

Sally finally cracked a smile. "If I tell you, I'll have to kill you."

"Funny."

"You think so when you say it. Besides, I can't believe you didn't know it."

"I suspected it. You knew it for sure. Who's your source?"

"Seriously, Gil, I can't tell you. You're a detective. I'm sure you can figure it out."

"Harry Clark," I concluded, looking away so she wouldn't betray his trust by giving it away with her eyes. "Did he tell you or did you overhear something? Don't answer that; it doesn't matter. So, is Harry in on it? Your opinion is all I'm asking for."

Sally shook her head. "Not willingly, I don't think. He likes you, Gil, despite the way you feel about him."

"My opinion of him has changed during this last year. Not completely, but in the right direction."

"Harry knows how valuable you are. The problem is, he's afraid of you. He knows you'd do a better job of being security manager than him."

"I don't know about that," I deferred. "I don't have any designs on his job."

"He doesn't know that. You know how it is — everyone thinks everyone else is out to get all they can as quickly as they can. They'd trample anyone in their way, and Harry figures you're no different."

"I just want to be left alone."

"You've got to admit, honey, it sure doesn't look that way. People who are content to be what and where they are usually aren't as outspoken as you."

Honey. She called me honey.

"To many people you come off as a grandstander," Sally added.

"That's not the case, and you know it."

"Yes, I do — well, for the most part. You do enjoy upstaging Theo. And that police captain — what's his name?"

"I don't say it in mixed company."

This was all almost too much to handle, at least in my present state. I rubbed my forehead, then wiped my hand slowly down my face. I couldn't think straight any longer. I was too tired.

"Look, Sally, can all this wait until Monday? I need some sleep, and I don't want to get it during the sermon tomorrow. Well, maybe I wouldn't mind — depends on the sermon. What I'm saying is —"

"You're tired. I can see that." She scooted next to me and began rubbing the back of my neck. I dropped my chin onto my chest and closed my eyes.

The warmth of the fire I'd built began to waft over me, and my thoughts turned chaotic and dreamlike as I became aware of the scent of Sally's perfume. I pictured her in her sweater, her hair loose and buoyant on her shoulders. My carnal mind filled with thoughts I didn't want, desires I'd suppressed before but that had assaulted me under much less volatile circumstances. I longed for Sally's embrace, the way I used to long for . . . Rachel's. But it wasn't Rachel I longed for now. She was a sweet memory, but that's all she was. Sally was the present, and Sally was my future, Lord willing.

My eyes opened, and I blinked them, unable to see clearly. I was on a sofa but was suddenly disoriented. The fire still burned, but the log was half-consumed. I was on my side, my head on a throw pillow, my shoes off, and I was covered by a blanket.

I sat up groggy and confused, a bad taste in my mouth. The pizza was gone, the coffee table clean. Only a piece of paper remained, a short, handwritten note.

Checking the clock over the mantel, I noticed that four hours had passed. I gently plucked the note from the table and moved it up and back until the writing came into focus.

"You fell asleep," I read aloud. "See you in church if you make it. Love, Sally."

I leaned back on the sofa and rested my neck on the arm, gazing up at the stylish acoustic ceiling with a sigh.

"Thank You, Lord," I whispered, "for saving me from myself." I slid all the way down onto the cushions and shut my eyes, listening to the crackling fire.

It wasn't just for you — it was for Sally too.

I gave God a wave, opened my eyes for a second, and glanced around the room, knowing He hadn't spoken in an audible voice, yet wondering just the same. I smiled and closed my eyes again and went back to sleep.

NINE

I woke again at 8:30. The fire was cold, the sun was up, and I was late. I threw off the covers and raced to the bathroom, showered, shaved, combed and brushed, and tossed on my best suit. I grabbed my Bible and ran out to the BMW, jumped in and cranked it over, and drove quickly to church without breaking any traffic laws.

Yeah, right.

When I got there Sally was standing at the curb, looking very anxious but relieved to see me. I parked in a stall near the front doors marked VISITORS ONLY. I figured I had missed enough Sundays lately, I was qualified.

"Glad you made it," Sally said with a smile, catching my arm at the elbow and pulling me gently toward the church doors. "Come on, I hate to be late."

"I hate you to be late too. Me I don't mind so much. You didn't have to wait out here, you know. I'd have found you."

"Shh."

We were nearing the doors, which were still open. Inside, the congregation was standing and thumbing through their hymnals. We found a seat and joined in the singing, then settled into the pew after the opening prayer. I crossed my legs, noticing that my right sock was brown. I thought that was odd since my suit was gray, so as discreetly as I could I checked the other sock a short while later. Dark blue. Oops.

Oh well, I'm only human.

Church let out at 10:30 after a rousing benediction of repetitious "amens," which followed a particularly penetrating sermon about the nature and penalty of sin.

"Boy, the pastor sure had most of these people pegged," I told Sally, sweeping my arm toward the rest of the congregation in the courtyard, most of whom were swarming around the coffee and muffin table.

"What about you?" Sally asked.

"Me? Oh, I don't want a muffin, but thanks anyway."

"I mean the sermon," she clarified, tilting her head down and peering at me over her glasses.

"Oh, yeah. Heh heh. He was right on." I smiled. "Seriously, it was good to be reminded that sin isn't just doing something the Bible says not to do. It's doing *anything* that falls short of God's glory. Even doing something that's not necessarily sin, if it's done in rebellion, becomes sin for the doer."

"Okay," Sally said. "I was just wondering if you were listening. A couple times there I thought you were asleep with your eyes open. During one stretch I don't think you blinked for a full minute."

Before I had a chance to comment on how she ought to be listening to the pastor instead of watching me blink, I spied a familiar face across the courtyard.

"Well, look there," I told Sally. "Over by the bush."

"Oh, my. Isn't that —"

"It sure is. I have to admit, I'm super-surprised."

"I'm not," said Sally. "Not in the light of all that's happened."

"Let's go greet our visitor," I suggested. "Stay close. I'll forge a path through the human jungle. If you fall too far behind, it'll close up behind me, and you'll be lost until Wednesday prayer meeting."

I headed pell-mell into the throng, almost at normal speed. I was good at this, did it all the time at the park. Halfway through I felt a hand clasp mine. It wasn't sticky, so I assumed it was Sally's and didn't look back or slow down.

Breaking free of the muffining masses, I caught and held my quarry's glance, giving a big smile in return.

"Good to see you," I said. "To what do we owe this auspicious occasion?"

"Gil? I didn't expect to see you here," said Michelle Yokoyama.

"That should be my line, shouldn't it?"

She gave me a courtesy laugh. "What I meant was, I didn't know this was your church."

"We've both gone here a long time," Sally said. "How are you doing, Miss Yokoyama? I'm sorry about what happened."

"Please, call me Michelle." She took Sally's hand, which had been extended in greeting. They both raised their free hands and enveloped each other in a kind of warm, supportive grasp. "Thank you for your concern. I'm a little flabbergasted by the suddenness of it all, of course. And I'm none too happy about losing my job. I put in a lot of years there. But on the whole it doesn't really surprise me. Jerry's one of those people who is very conscious of the threat others pose to his security, even if it's only imagined."

"He's a paranoid schizo-incompetent," I suggested.

Michelle glanced at me, and I expected her usual conciliatory demurring, but she said nothing. So I added, "And an ignorant jerk."

"Gil," Sally cautioned, "you shouldn't say that at church."

"He's right," Michelle told her. "Unfortunately."

"What are you going to do?" Sally asked, then before Michelle could respond added, "I'm sorry. I don't mean to pry. I'm just concerned."

"That's okay, Sally. I don't mind. I haven't decided, actually. They gave me a substantial severance check."

"No chance of appeal?" I asked.

"This isn't like civil service, Gil. They can pretty much do as they want."

"What excuse — er, reason did they give?"

"Gil, that's personal," Sally said.

"I know, Sally, but whatever they told her, it's garbage. Jerry had no grounds, and even if it is private enterprise, there's usually a reason for firing someone. Even if it's false, they had to give her a reason." I turned to Michelle. "Sorry. I didn't mean to talk about you like you're not here. You don't have to tell me. I'm just steamed, that's all. It's not like I need another reason to dislike Jerry."

"That doesn't sound very Christian," Michelle observed with a wry grin.

I turned to Sally. "I hate it when people are right like that. Okay, Michelle, I had that coming. Forget I said it."

"That's okay, Gil, I feel the same way. In fact, I'm flattered you feel that way about it."

"It just frosts me how much that goofball keeps getting away with."

"Nobody said life is supposed to be fair," Sally reminded me.

"I don't want fair, Sally, I want it to be *just*. There's a difference."

"It's not fair or just," Michelle said with a shrug. "It's like the relocation centers, remember? They were neither fair nor just."

"Psalm 84," I said. "Blessed men go through valleys of weeping. The point being, there are valleys of weeping for God's children, but we will go *through* them, not stay in them."

"Interesting," Michelle said. "To answer your question, they said I no longer fit in their plans for the future."

"Hogwash!" I said.

Sally agreed with me, although she phrased it a trifle more eloquently. "That's a shovelful of malarkey."

"Sally," I chastened, "I don't think you can say *malarkey* at church."

Michelle grinned and shrugged. "I tend to agree with both of you. But there's not much I can do about it. *Giri*, Gil," she said, using a Japanese word she'd explained to me on an earlier occasion.

"Contentment, making the most of every situation. Building a garden in the desert. Yes, I remember."

"I can find another job. There are other theme parks."

"How about a department store chain or something like that?" I suggested.

She nodded. "That's a good idea. Or maybe I'll do like you — get a job in a related field but well below my skill level and earning capacity. Like a sales clerk's position at the perfume counter."

"You trying to tell me something?" I asked, folding my arms.

"Yes. Go back to the P.D. That's what you really want to do, isn't it?"

"I don't know. Maybe. It's what I wanted a while back. Now I'm not so sure. Besides, they won't have me. Capt. Fitzgerald would put the kibosh to it before the ink dried on my application."

"Oh, so Capt. Fitzgerald is the hurdle."

"No, he's the twelve-foot wall with razor wire on the top and armed guards in towers."

"Oh, I wouldn't go that far."

There was a twinkle in her eye, and the way she said it made me wonder if she knew something I didn't.

"Why not?"

"Oh," said Michelle. "No reason."

I let it go at that, for the time being. I knew her well enough to know she'd say more if she wanted to. There was meaning in her voice, but I didn't want to guess at it and get my hopes up, for fear of being wrong. Besides, I could call Theo later. Thinking of him prompted me to ask, "So, where's Theo anyway? And for that matter, what brings you here, since it apparently wasn't to see me? I'm glad you came, of course — I'm just surprised."

"Well, to be honest," she said slowly, dropping her head slightly in a classic oriental act of humility that I'd never seen from her before, "getting fired has made me think twice about a lot of things. Theo and I have been discussing the Bible lately — some of the things you've been telling him and some of the things he's been reading. He wanted to come but got called into work in the middle of the night. Some gang shooting across town." She paused, then added with an embarrassed smile, "He called me to tell me he couldn't make it. We weren't together."

"You don't have to explain yourself to us," Sally assured.

"Under the circumstances, I thought I should," Michelle said.

"Gangs," I said with an attitude. "Another good reason not to go back into law enforcement."

Sally changed the subject. "So, Michelle, are you going into church, or do you want to go to adult Bible study with us? It's about time to start."

I glanced back at the muffin table, which looked like a wildebeest carcass after the vultures had flown off.

"I thought I'd go in to church today," Michelle said. "Maybe next week I'll come earlier so I can do both."

"That would be wonderful!" said Sally. "Well, so long. We're so glad to see you. God will work everything out, I know."

"Yes, I believe that."

I smiled and winked. "Tell Theo hi for me. I'll give him a call sometime. I hope he enjoyed the fishing trip."

"He did. Said it was one of the best trips he's ever been on. Totally relaxing."

I smiled. "It had its moments."

TEN

I walked Sally to her car after Sunday school. Our teacher had been a trifle long-wind — er, filled to overflowing with the Word, so church had already let out and many of the people had driven off. Michelle was one of them. At least I didn't see her or her car anywhere. I wondered what she thought of the sermon and said as much to Sally.

"God's in control," she said. "If He's working on her — and I'll bet He is, the way she came here without being invited — then she'll get out of it what He wants her to."

"His Word was certainly taught today," I said. "Uh oh."

"Uh oh? His Word was taught today, uh oh?"

"Don't look now, but here comes our favorite matchmaker."

"Where?" Sally asked as she craned her neck to see.

"I told you not to look," I chastised. "Now we're committed."

"Hi, Joyce," Sally greeted cheerfully. It'll always be a mystery to me how women can act charmed so easily.

I pasted on a grinning mouth unaccompanied by smiling eyes. The old gal was okay every now and then, but I didn't want another Sunday dinner listening to her and her husband complaining about their aches and pains and which brand of goo keeps their dentures in place better, illustrated by a visual demonstration. It was just hard to tell her no. Well, it wasn't actually hard to tell her, she just never understood the word and expected you to show up anyway. I wished Sally and I already had an engagement.

"How are you children today?" she asked fawningly.

"Fine," Sally said.

"I have a loose tooth," I said.

"Gil . . ." Sally warned sternly through a clenched smile while continuing to look at Mrs. Stevens.

It didn't matter what I said. The woman wasn't listening.

"Mr. Stevens and I were just saying to each other how much we'd like to take you to lunch."

Translation: Mr. Stevens didn't know anything about it, and Mrs. Stevens wanted to meet us there and let us pay our own way. "Take you" meant neither "drive you" nor "treat you" to Mrs. Stevens.

"Well, that's very kind of you," Sally said. "We'd love to."

Translation: Sally wouldn't mind, but Gil would rather get a paper cut on his lips. I scrunched my eyes shut, forcing myself not to think of all the terrible names I wanted to call my darling at that particular moment.

"But I'm afraid we won't be able to today," Sally continued. "We already have plans."

My eyes popped open. Had I just heard what I thought I heard? Had Sally just fibbed?

"We're going on a picnic."

"Yeah, a picnic," I echoed, certain my nose had just grown several inches. I gave Sally a puzzled glance.

"Oh, isn't that nice," Mrs. Stevens said. "Well, you two love birds have a good time now. We'll take a rain check on that lunch." She waved and padded off toward her car where her husband waited as he patiently blew the horn.

To Sally I whispered, "How about a cold day in you-know-where check?"

"Gil, don't talk that way," she scolded.

"Look who's talking, Pinocchio. What's all this about a picnic?"

"Don't you think that would be fun?"

"That's not fair. How am I supposed to answer that?"

"That you think it would be a blast."

I thought it over, then shrugged. "I've never been big on picnics. I don't like eating outside, the breeze blows your napkin, ants and bugs attack you — I don't even like patio tables at Italian restaurants."

"You get to sit on a blanket with me under a shady tree."

"Sandwiches or chicken?" I replied quickly.

"It's all ready, Mr. Stick-in-the-Mud. You just have to follow me to my place, and we'll pick it up."

All ready? She had this thing planned all along, the little . . . *Wait a minute,* I told myself. *You think she's great, you'd rather be with her than anyone else on the planet — except maybe Olivia Newton-John — and she obviously wants to be with you. Go for it, Gilbert!*

"Oh, okay," I said reluctantly. "Since you've gone to all that trouble, I suppose I can force myself to have a good time."

Sally closed one eye and scrutinized me carefully. I think that's how she activated her X-ray vision to read my thoughts. "Don't put yourself out," she said, then smiled. "See you at my place."

"Want me to get anything?"

"A new attitude maybe."

"Besides that."

"Can you pick up some chips?"

"Okay. See you in a few minutes."

As she drove off I watched her for a few seconds, more unsure of myself than ever. I loved her and wanted to be with her, but something inside me was making it difficult, making me say goofy things, things that could cause a problem — *would* cause a problem with a woman who was less a woman than Sally.

Was I trying to self-destruct, to ruin the relationship subconsciously because of Rachel? That was nuts, but . . .

My falling asleep the night before — did that bother Sally? Did she take it personally, like maybe she thought she'd bored me or I didn't want to be with her? Maybe she took it as rejection. It wasn't that, not at all. Truth is, I wanted to be with her in the worst way, and I do mean the worst way. But it wouldn't be right, even for a couple of experienced adults like us.

Maybe we could talk about it. Sally had always struck me as a down-to-earth, practical woman. Surely, as a sensible woman — and a Christian — she could talk about it.

I drove to the convenience store and bought a couple bags of chips — regular potato chips and some salt-and-vinegar flavored chips, the kind that clear your sinuses and make your jaw muscles quiver.

Of course, it could be that her divorce had affected her more than I realized, perhaps even more than she realized. I mean, it must be quite a jolt to be cast aside for someone else. Sally was a real "with it" woman, but maybe now that she was on the brink of something she hadn't had in quite a while, maybe she, too, was having second thoughts.

And there are differing opinions within the church on divorced people remarrying, and that could be weighing on her mind. Although both the Old and New Testaments discuss the issue, the Bible is ambiguous regarding many aspects of the problem. Are the victims of a divorce — those who don't want one but it's forced upon them — prohibited from remarrying? What about people who divorce and remarry before being saved? In Old Testament times it really wasn't an issue when adultery was involved, because the offending spouse would be stoned to death. The remaining person was obviously free to remarry because his or her spouse was dead.

Personally, I believe the Bible is ambiguous because of grace. God doesn't want us to get bogged down in legalism, but to live in the freedom of His grace. Not freedom to continue sinning, but to know we're forgiven and to walk in the Spirit. We aren't to divorce on the assumption that He'll forgive us — that would be licentiousness. But if we're divorced, we can know we're forgiven and can vow from that day forward to be a one-woman man or a one-man woman.

I told myself to be careful, not so cavalier with the sarcasm, to be aware of her mindset if I could, to read her emotions and try to dovetail in with them. And above all, to do my best to understand what made her tick.

Then I'd find a cure for cancer and end world hunger.

Who was I kidding? All I could do was be myself, just not so much of it all the time.

She was waiting outside for me when I drove up, a blanket over one arm and a basket in the other. With the noon sun reflecting off her face, I could almost forget it was only 60 degrees. The clothes she'd bundled up in reminded me of that.

"Not fair," I protested as I opened the door for her.

She handed me the blanket and basket and got in.

"What?" she asked.

"You're all casual, I'm still in a suit."

"So we'll go by your place and change. I'm not in a hurry."

I put the picnic basket in the backseat,

drank in a surreptitious look at her profile, with her straight nose, Reba McIntyre lips, and weather-blushed cheeks, then jumped in, my heart suddenly banging on the inside of my chest wall, and cranked the BMW into life.

"Comfy?" Sally asked as I returned to the car in jeans, tennis shoes, and a leather coat, a Christmas present to myself the previous year.

"Perfect. Where to?"

"The park has a nice picnic area."

"Which park?" I asked suspiciously.

"Ours, of course — the one where we work."

"Oh, good gr—" I checked myself. "Okay, Sal, that's fine." I revved the motor and let out the clutch.

She was right of course. The picnic grounds adjacent to one of the parking areas was pleasant. With plenty of trees, winding paths, a Japanese koi pond, and two hours of free parking to accommodate shoppers in the marketplace outside the fence of the theme park itself, it was available to anyone anytime for free.

It was a quiet place and not so close to the park that the clanking of machinery, the whine of roller coaster wheels on their tracks, and the scream of park guests — and their kids — intruded on the solitude.

We ate and enjoyed quiet conversation, most of it insignificant. I told her the high points of my adventures in the mountains, but while strolling hand-in-hand through the woods, she brought up Mrs. Potter.

"I've been trying not to think about it, Gil," she confessed, "but I can't help it. I'm worried."

"I understand. It's a puzzle, to be sure."

"If she'd keeled over dead at home or even at her desk, it wouldn't be so difficult. I mean, she's getting on in years, and even though she's spry and plenty active, I still wouldn't have been surprised if she'd died suddenly."

"Maybe she did," I suggested. "Just not where anyone knew her. Like maybe she was out of town and got hit by a truck, and her purse was dragged off so they couldn't identify her, or something like that. I know, that doesn't sound too encouraging, but it could happen. They've pretty much ruled out that she just decided on a whim not to show up at work ever again."

"Call Theo, Gil. Would you? Have him check it out."

"What can he do that hasn't already been

done? Unless she led a secret life as a circus performer, all her known haunts have been checked."

"Maybe security has heard something recently," Sally said hopefully. "They might have tried to call me but weren't able to reach me." Her face brightened. "That's it! I'll bet they know. Let's go check."

"Okay, Sal, okay. I'll put the stuff in the car, and we'll walk over there."

Sally turned and rushed back to the picnic area where we'd left the blanket and nearly empty basket. She snatched the blanket up and shook it, wadding it in her arms as she headed for the car. I followed with the basket. The car loaded and secured, she took my hand and led me across the way, through the open-air stores, fast-food stops, and guest relations rooms to the security office.

Inside, we waved to the dispatcher, sitting behind a window at the radio console, and pushed our way through a door. The squad room was full of uniformed and plainclothes officers listening to the swing shift sergeant finish briefing. We stood quietly at the back of the room.

"Those of you working the main gate area tonight, and all perimeter units as well, and anyone who might be walking by the ticket booths on your way to a break or something, keep an eye out for the Ticket Booth Bandit. The P.D. passed along a teletype they got on him today. He's been hitting theme parks all over the Southland and seems to be working his way toward us.

"His M.O. is pretty simple. He rides a bicycle up to the booth, usually when there is no line, points a gun at the clerk through the glass, and demands money. He gets it and rides off, probably to a waiting car, and is long gone before the cops get there.

"If you encounter him, don't be a hero. Remember, he's armed, and we don't know but that he has accomplices. Follow him from a safe distance if you can, get a good description of him and his car — obviously a license plate would be best — but don't force his hand. If you have to, back off and let him go. Just be a good witness and no more."

He passed out copies of the teletype containing the guy's description, then added, "He doesn't really have a pattern. He'll strike anytime any day. The only giveaway, such as it is, is the bicycle. Oh, and he wears sunglasses and one of those tight-fitting bicycle caps — yellow with a bunch of writing on it. Okay, people, put on your smiles and go to work."

The men and women of park security got

up mumbling and laughing and filed out, some of them greeting Sally and me. When they were gone, Sgt. Howard came over.

"Gil, Sally, what brings you two here on a Sunday evening?"

"Sally's worried about Mrs. Potter," I said. "We both are," I added when Sally took my hand and squeezed it. She didn't let go. It was no longer a secret that she and I were an item. Harry Clark didn't like it, but he'd just have to get over it.

"We were hoping you'd heard something," Sally said hopefully.

Sgt. Howard shook his head. "Sorry, not a thing. She hasn't turned up. No clues. I'll have dispatch put a note on the console to call you when we hear anything, Sally. I wish I had more to tell you."

"That's okay," she said quietly, the air let out of her hope.

"Thanks, Art," I said, and the sergeant nodded and retired into his office. "Come on, Sally," I said quietly. "Let's go home."

She nodded sadly, and I put my arm around her shoulder.

"It'll be okay," I comforted. "God's in control. He knows where she is." I led her outside, and we retraced our steps toward the parking lot.

Passing a large floral display, we watched

188

an elderly employee — one of the original park employees — watering the flowers, something he was paid a hefty wage to do. He was one of the leftovers from the park's inception, a crony of Mr. Golden's who didn't have any particular skills except losing at poker to Golden and being his chum since their youth. Being a loyal person, Golden had kept this guy and the others like him around as long as they wanted, paying them well enough to never want to leave.

This tradition had been carried on by the group who took over the park after the childless Golden's death. They had little choice — it was in his will. Mrs. Potter and Al "Pop" Miller were the only remaining original employees.

He noticed us eyeing him and gave us a smile and a wave.

"Evening, Al," Sally said.

"Good evening, Miss Sally, Mr. Beckman. Beautiful day, isn't it?"

"Yes, lovely."

"You do good work, Pop," I told him.

"Thanks, Mr. Beckman. I love taking care of these flowers up here the most. Mr. Ozawa does a good job, and ever since they hired him, he's taught me how to make them look great. It's too bad about him."

"Being fired, you mean?" I asked.

"Yeah. Doesn't make any sense. He did a good job, and . . . Well, truth be told, they should've got rid of me first. He knows so much more than I do. All I can really do is water and fuss."

"That's important," Sally observed.

"Oh, sure. But anyone can do that. Mr. Ozawa, he was right in the middle of a project. I can't figure out why they picked now to do it. Mr. Golden would have never done such a thing."

I reflected on that. Why *had* they fired him? They said it was because of downsizing, but there were plenty of people who could have been jettisoned way before Ozawa. And Pop was right — Ozawa was doing a major landscaping project. Could it be because of his relationship to Hiromoto or Michelle? That was only speculation, but what other reason could there be? And if true, what did it mean?

"Well, you take care, Al," I said. "Keep up the —" I snapped my fingers and stopped walking, pulling Sally back to me.

"What is it?" she asked.

"Al was outside Mrs. Potter's office the morning she disappeared. He was watering the hanging planters that line her porch."

Without waiting for her to respond, I went back to Pop Miller, who had been watching us quizzically since my self-interrupted farewell.

"Pop, do you recall the day recently when I spoke to you outside Jerry Opperman's office?"

He scratched his forehead.

"When you almost squirted me with the hose?" I added.

"Oh, yeah. Sure do."

"That was the day Mrs. Potter disappeared."

"It was?" He shook his head. "That just don't make any sense. Known Mrs. Potter fifty years. Mr. Potter too, until he died. She's a good woman. Sent me a birthday card every year, never missed one. I hope she's okay. I remember one time me and Ozzie . . . Mr. Golden, you know . . . We were sittin' around in his apartment, having tea and a cigar — he didn't drink, but he had a nice stash of cigars, didn't even need a humidor where he kept 'em. Anyway, the phone rings, and he ignores it, and pretty soon she comes down and starts yellin' at him —"

"Excuse me, Pop," I interrupted. "But can you tell me about that morning, the one last week?"

"You went in," said Miller thoughtfully. "You went in, then you came out, then Mr.

Opperman went in — that's all I know. I left right about then."

"While you were there, did you see anything unusual? How long had you been there?"

"Oh, forty-five minutes maybe. Just long enough to water all the flowers, pick off the brown petals."

"You didn't see or hear anything strange?"

"No, nothing out of the ordinary. Mrs. Potter came in early —"

"What? She came in?" Sally asked.

"Yes, ma'am. Around 7:30, just when I got there. She said, 'Good morning, Al' and went inside. Then about a half-hour later you came by, Mr. Beckman."

"She wasn't there when I went in," I told him. "The office was empty."

He looked down at the ground, perplexed. "No, I'm sure about it. She went in before you and never came out. She had to be inside."

"I know I asked you already, but did you see or hear anything — anything at all? Even regular noises? Please, Mr. Miller, think. It's important."

"I reckon it must be." He rubbed his chin while looking at his shoes.

"Nope," he concluded after a few seconds. "Just a crackling sound."

"Crackling sound?"

"Yeah, you know, like a . . . like a fireplace with green wood in it, or stiff paper being wadded up. Only it wasn't very loud."

"Do you consider it a normal sound or unusual?"

"Never thought about it. Depends on what it was, don't it?"

"It was a quiet sound, you say?"

"No, not quiet really. It was like a loud noise faraway, not a quiet noise up close."

"How about inside the office? Could it have come from there?"

"Hmmm." He stroked his chin some more. "I suppose so."

"I don't understand," Sally said to me. "There's no fireplace in there, and you wouldn't be able to hear paper being crumpled from outside, even if you were on the porch."

"You're right," Miller said. "That's not what it was — that's just what it sounded like."

"Okay, Pop, thanks," I said. "Come on, Sally." I grabbed her hand and pulled her toward the parking lot.

"Good-bye, Al," Sally called. "And thank you."

"Good-bye, kids. And good luck."

ELEVEN

"Where are we going now?" Sally asked as she double-timed to keep up with me.

"Hollie's Hut. I need to think."

"Hollie's Hut? Exactly what do you think about at Hollie's Hut?"

"It's where I do some of my best work," I explained.

"And you're taking me there?"

"I'm talking about thinking, not Hollie."

"I'll bet."

I unlocked the car and packed her in. "Besides, we haven't had dessert yet."

Hollie saw us coming and met us at the door.

"Well, well, well, if it isn't my long-lost former heart throb."

"I think it isn't," I suggested, ever mindful of Sally's feelings. Hollie didn't appear too concerned, however, and gave me an impromptu hug and kiss so quickly I didn't have a chance to enjoy it. My face turned crimson, and I feigned shyness. My carnal instinct was to grab her and bend her over backward like they used to do in the movies. But my sense of propriety — and self-pres-

ervation — held on, and I gave Sally a surreptitious apology.

"So that's why you wanted to come here,"
she said dryly.

But Sally needn't have worried. Hollie
greeted her too, then held her hand up.

"Check this out!" she declared, and we
both widened our eyes at a rock the size of
a healthy strawberry.

"Home Shopping Club?" I guessed.

Hollie ignored me. Sally moved in for a
closer look.

"You're engaged?" she asked the restau-
rateur.

"You better believe it, honey! Got this a
week ago."

"Kinda sudden, don't you think?" I said,
hurt obvious in my voice. "I thought it'd
take a little longer for you to get over me."

"You?" Hollie waved me off with an exaggerated flip of her hand. "You're ancient
history, darling, and I do mean ancient. That
was a good-bye kiss, to let you know what
you're gonna be missing."

"So who's the really lucky —" I hesitated,
catching Sally's sudden glare out of the corner of my eye. "I mean, who's the gentle-
man?"

"You may know him. He works at the
park. Of course, around here who doesn't?

He just got a big promotion too, I might add."

Sally and I said it simultaneously.

"Dave Whelan?"

"No, of course not. He's engaged to his former secretary, Lois Schilling. Come on, don't give me those looks. You knew that, didn't you?"

"I've been on vacation," I told her.

"Oh. Well, anyway, I'm marrying the man who took his place as head of Rides — Tim Carter."

"Of course," Sally said with a smile. "We know him. He's a real nice man. Good-looking too." I gave Sally a raised-eyebrow look, but she ignored it.

"I had no idea," I told her. "I think it's great. I'm just a little taken aback, that's all."

"Well," Hollie admitted slowly, "it hasn't been all that long that we've been, you know, serious. He's come in now and then for a few years, just like you. It's only recently that we started seeing each other. But it's been grand, every minute of it."

"When are you taking the plunge?" I asked.

"Summer. I want a June wedding. I know that's kind of silly for someone my age."

"Not at all," Sally said dreamily. "I think it's neat."

Suddenly I began to get a little warm.

"Well, shoot, that's enough about me. You two came here to eat, I presume. Your regular table is open, Gil. Have at it."

We took our seats, and Angela came by immediately with menus and coffee. We ordered pie, and while we waited, Sally brought up the conversation I'd had with Pop Miller.

"So what was it you came here to think about?" Sally asked as we sipped our coffee.

"Those sounds Pop Miller heard. I think that might be the key to the whole thing."

"What do you think th   r   ight have been?"

"Something electrical, it sounds like. But exactly what it was, and what, if any, relevance it had to Mrs. Potter's disappearance, I can't say."

"Why did we have to come here to think about it?"

"I seem to do a better job thinking when I have something to eat in front of me, and Hollie's Hut is the closest place to the park. It's also good food." I paused. "And the door greetings can't be beat."

"Back to the subject, Casanova."

"Okay, okay. You heard Pop say Mrs. Potter came in that morning about 7:30. Pretty much normal time, I'd wager. You see? She arrived like always, but a half-hour later she was gone even though she didn't leave."

"You're not making sense, Gil."

"I'm not trying to right now. Those are just the facts. What we have to do is make some sense of it, find a scenario that fits the facts. Okay, listen — she came in but didn't leave — at least by the front door. But when I came in, she wasn't there. There's either another way out or she's still in there. Or was that morning at least."

"Where? You looked everywhere that morning. You said so."

"But I wasn't looking for Mrs. Potter who had vanished under normal circumstances. I was looking for a normal Mrs. Potter whom I expected to be in her office or in one of the other adjacent rooms."

"Did you look in Jerry's office?"

"I had no reason to."

"She could have been in there."

"Yes, but if she was in there, she would've come out when I called. If that's the case, she was in there against her will and couldn't come out. If that's true, then Jerry knows what happened to her." I shook my head. "Doesn't make any sense. Besides, what reason could he possibly have for harming her? She's known all about him all these years and never said a bad word about him to anyone."

"She's loyal, that's for sure," Sally agreed.

"Even to someone she doesn't like."

"That's conjecture on your part, Gil. Just because you don't like him doesn't mean Mrs. Potter doesn't. I'm sure there are lots of people who like Jerry just fine."

"Simpletons," I muttered. "People who don't know any better. Forrest Gump wanna-be's. Or those who've profited by him. They may not actually like him, of course, but they'd never admit it, not as long as he's in power."

Our dessert came, great heaping mounds of pie with vanilla ice cream á la mode we hadn't ordered.

"You're too black and white, Gil," Sally scolded when Angela was out of earshot. "You know, occasionally there is middle ground, people who don't have an opinion one way or the other."

"Fence sitters," I said. "Lukewarm. The kind God spews out of His mouth."

"Excellent mealtime conversation, Gil."

"Sorry, but it's true. What if the whole world was afraid to commit? There'd never be any change, much less progress."

"How does liking Jerry Opperman relate to the invention of the cotton gin?"

"Look, if no one takes a stand on people like Jerry Opperman, they stay in power. Take Capt. Fitzgerald from the P.D., for example. He's the kind of guy who is so afraid of making a wrong decision that he won't make any. He'll always say he's waiting for more information. And when he gets more, it's not enough. He might find out something else tomorrow that would affect his decision, so he'll put it off and put it off until it no longer matters or is too late. He considers it being open-minded, but it's just the lack of ability to make a decision."

Angela came by with more coffee. "How's the pie, kids? Okay?"

"Yes," Sally said. "Very tasty."

"Excellent," I echoed. "As always."

Angela smiled as if she'd made the pie herself, then twirled away to attend to another table.

"Let's get back to Mrs. Potter," I said. "We need to find out what that noise was. Maybe someone who works at the park can tell us."

"Like who?"

"Like Dave Whelan. He knows the rides and everything electrical at the park. And he's helped you before."

"Good idea. And while we're there we can offer our congratulations."

TWELVE

A surprised Dave Whelan answered the door.

"Gil, Sally, I . . . uh . . . is everything okay?"

"Just fine," I said. "We heard about your engagement and wanted to stop by and congratulate you. Sorry we didn't call first."

"Oh, no, that's okay. Please, come on in." He stepped back, and we entered the upscale tract home in a Volvo-filled neighborhood. "This is quite a surprise. I wasn't expecting you two."

Who were you expecting? I wondered.

"I imagine not," I said. "Sally and I were having a bite at Hollie's Hut, and she mentioned that you and Lois had gotten engaged."

"Oh, yes, Hollie. Nice lady. Do you know her?"

Dave put the question to me, but Sally said dryly, "You could say that."

"I guess she and Lois are pretty good friends," Dave said.

"Hollie is friends with a lot of people from the park," I noted.

"We're so happy for you and Lois," Sally said.

"Yes," I echoed. "Congratulations. You know, I always thought you two were —"

Sally elbowed me in the side.

Dave laughed. "Was it that obvious?"

"No, not at all," I said. "I'm just a good detective, remember?"

"Well, we've been going out for a couple of years, actually. But I didn't want to jeopardize either of our positions, so we kept it secret. But now since she's no longer my secretary, we can be open about it."

"Well, we think it's great," Sally said.

"Thank you, thank you both. I — please, I'm forgetting my manners. Let's go in the living room, take a load off."

He ushered us in, and we crossed the immaculate off-white carpet to the huge pastel sofa that looked like it had never been sat on. I dusted off the back of my pants before easing myself onto the edge of the cushion.

"I'm a little surprised to see you both," he went on when we were settled, taking a chair on the other side of the coffee table. "I wasn't expecting visitors, and when I saw it was you two, I . . . Well, I thought there was some serious problem at the park — like an accident or something. You know, with both of you being in security and everything, plus the way things have been going lately."

"I can see how you'd think that," I said. "Sorry, we didn't mean to alarm you. We didn't think of that." The reason we didn't is because it wouldn't have happened that way. Any news like that would be telephoned, and if it was so bad that a personal visit was required, somebody higher up than a security guard and a secretary would deliver it. But on the other hand, the part of the brain that deals in logical thought usually shuts down briefly when one is surprised, so I guess his initial reaction didn't necessarily mean anything sinister.

"Well, I'm certainly glad this is social," Dave said with an exhale. "There's been enough bad news at the park in recent months."

"But good news too," Sally said. "Congratulations on your promotion."

"Thank you." Dave's expression didn't light up, and his next comment explained it. "I'm really sorry about Michelle. I wish my success could have come another way."

"Us too," I said. "We're happy about your promotion, but sorry it had to be at Michelle's expense. We like you both."

"Yes," Sally agreed.

"Thank you. I'm afraid some people aren't going to be so magnanimous."

"They'll blame you, that's for sure," I said. "But don't worry about them — they'll get over it." I noticed a small modern sculpture on the end table next to me, a bizarre Picasso-like thing, completely unrecognizable, but with a small light in it to give it an eerie glow. I reached over absentmindedly to turn it toward me so I could see it from a better angle, but just as I was about to make contact I got a shock of static electricity.

"Whoa!" I said. "It bit."

"You shouldn't have touched it," scolded Sally.

"Sorry," Dave said. "New carpet, and I just vacuumed."

Sally leaned over and whispered, "Keep your hands to yourself, Gil. If you break anything, you'll be paying for it for years."

I smiled at Dave and folded my hands in my lap.

Sally took us back to the conversation. "It was very fortuitous for you and Lois," she noted without explaining further what she meant. "I know she has mixed emotions about her new position too. Appreciative and honored, yet wishing it hadn't been necessary."

"So true. Isn't it terrible about Mrs. Potter? Personally, I would've kept the position open, but Jerry wanted someone to fill it right away — only temporary, of course, until Mrs. Potter returns. But Lois is certainly qualified."

That stung. Not me, so much, but Sally. At least it should have. Sally was just as qualified as Lois and had been there longer. But Sally hung out with me, and Jerry knew it. At that moment it really hit home how the things I did and said had a direct impact on the lives of other people — innocent people who were not directly involved in my situations and whose only crime was being my friend. A sense of regret passed through me, and I was at first a little wary to even look at Sally, knowing — just knowing — she was thinking it too. But after a moment I steeled myself and cast her an apologetic glance, ready to mouth the words, "I'm sorry."

But if she was thinking it, or if she felt any regret or anger or disappointment, her face didn't betray it. She didn't look at me but continued to regard Whelan with wide-eyed admiration and approval.

Which made me feel like an even bigger jerk. If I were her, I'd be pouting so much you could set a dinner plate on my bottom lip. Right then and there I made a momentous and irrevocable decision about my future with Sally Foster.

But Dave was still talking about Lois.

"Jerry said he needed a secretary to run interference for him, so with me taking

Michelle's spot, where there was already a secretary in place, it just seemed to make sense to put Lois in Mrs. Potter's spot. Jerry was certainly relieved. He spent the first few days alone, locked in his office."

"That's not unusual," I noted wryly.

Whelan smiled. "I suppose not. But he wouldn't answer the phone and came out only for meetings and to get lunch, which he usually took back to the office to eat. I never realized how much he ate until I saw him carry a tray back."

"He's pretty shaken up by this, I would imagine," Sally interjected.

"Seems to be more nervous than usual," Dave admitted.

"Speaking of Mrs. Potter," I declared before the conversation could overshoot the off-ramp, "we heard the strangest thing and wondered if maybe you could explain it."

"Me?" Dave's eyebrows raised.

"Yeah. You know about everything mechanical and electric in the park."

"What's that have to do with Mrs. Potter?"

"I was talking to someone today who was outside the administration office the morning she disappeared." I had no intention of telling him that she'd been seen at work that day.

"A suspect?" Dave asked.

"More like a witness."

"A witness. Just who was this witness?"

"Oh, one of the gardeners. He said he heard a strange noise come from her office, like a crackling sound. Kind of a snap crackle pop —"

"Was he eating Rice Krispies at the time?" Dave asked with a grin.

I chuckled and wished I'd said it. "Good one. No, but the sound was something like that. He said it was like stiff paper being crumpled or green wood in a fire. Can you think of anything that might make a noise like that?"

"Do you think it's important? I don't see how that could have anything to do with her disappearance, do you?"

"Don't know. One thing I've learned over the years, no clue is too small to be insignificant. That sound is out of the ordinary, at least for that area, which makes it important in light of the circumstances. It might be nothing, but you never know."

"Yes," Dave said pensively, "I see. He closed his eyes and imagined he was taking a mental tour of the park, hearing the sounds made by the rides. Sally and I settled back and looked at each other as we waited, and I suddenly realized we were holding hands.

Several thoughts converged on my mind, not all of them wholesome, and I fought them all off to concentrate on my questioning of the senior vice president. After no more than a minute he lifted his head.

"Could it be electrical?"

I shrugged. "It could be anything."

"How about the time portals in the Time Machine?"

I knit my brow, and he explained. "You know, where the cart passes through and the strobe lights flash?"

"Oh, yeah, of course." I snapped my fingers. "Strobe lights flash, accompanied by electric crackling and popping, just as my witness described."

Dave said, "That's the only thing I can think of that sounds like that, unless a transformer on a nearby power pole blew. But we'd've known about that. It would've affected the operation of the park, even if only for a few seconds."

"May I use your phone?" I asked suddenly.

"Huh? Oh, sure. There's one in the kitchen, that way." He pointed.

I left Sally to converse with Whelan and hustled to the kitchen, a large room with pure white cupboards and tile, a center island containing every conceivable appliance, and everything as immaculate as the living room. In fact, nothing looked like it'd ever been used, except for the coffeemaker. I couldn't resist, and before grabbing the phone, I peeked into the trash compactor. Just as I thought — take-out cartons from a Chinese restaurant.

I phoned park security and asked for Sgt. Howard. He listened to my request, set the receiver down, then returned in a few minutes.

"No, he's gone," Howard reported.

"Can you give me his home number?"

He could and did, and in another minute I had Pop Miller on the line.

"Pop, this is Gil Beckman. We spoke earlier in the marketplace."

"Sure, I remember. Whatcha need?"

"About that strange noise you heard . . . you've ridden the Time Machine, haven't you?"

"Plenty of times. For me it's like going back to my childhood." He hooted and snorted at his joke. I was beginning to feel like everyone else's straight man.

"You know that sound when you move through the strobe lights?"

"The time portals? Sure."

"Was the sound you heard like that?"

There was a brief silence. Then he said,

"You know, it *was* like that. Not as long or as loud but very similar. You don't think I'd've heard that so far away, do you?"

"No, Pop, I don't. Listen, you've been a big help. Thanks."

"Anytime, Mr. Beckman."

I hung up and considered what I knew. Mrs. Potter had come to work that morning but hadn't been seen leaving. Either she didn't or had gone out another way. Jerry might have a back way to his office, but if she'd used it, she would've been seen by someone. And if she did it of her own accord and by chance was unseen, where'd she go? If she was taken out against her will, I doubt she would've gone quietly. Even if she did cooperate, that's at least two people who would likely have been seen by someone, since at that hour the park is swarming with people getting ready for opening two hours later.

So, somehow she had to still be in there somewhere.

Also, there had been an electrical sound, brief but staccato-like, something associated with heavy electrical current but not a good connection — no, a good connection but . . . pulsating. That was it! — pulsating electricity.

I stood up straight as the hair on the back

of my neck raised, as though charged with electricity. I thought about that goofy electric sculpture in the living room and my recent conversation with Whelan, and the picture suddenly became clearer. Not crystal, because too many elements were missing. But now I was certain about what had happened to Mrs. Potter. Somewhat certain, at least.

I knew who, thanks to Dave, and I knew how. What I didn't know was why and, most importantly, where she was now. Nor did I know if she was still alive. For that I could only hope and pray.

"Thank You, Lord," I said out loud, glancing toward the illuminated ceiling. "And please . . . let this not be in vain."

Hurrying back into the living room, I apologized for taking so long and grabbed Sally by the hand, helping her gently off the sofa.

"Dave, thanks for your hospitality. We really need to run. Again, congratulations to you and Lois. I'll bet she loves the kitchen." I grabbed his hand and shook it. "We'll let ourselves out. Watch out, Sally, don't shuffle your feet. This carpet'll kill you."

"Th-thank you, Dave," Sally stammered. "All my best to both of you. Be sure to let us know when the wedding is."

"Yeah, we'll get you a toaster," I said.

"Thanks," a bewildered Dave Whelan said weakly as he watched us leave.

Sally waited until we were on our way in the BMW before speaking, then asked the obvious.

"Where are we going? You know something, don't you?"

"I think, I don't know." I shifted down for a hard right and accelerated through the corner. "What was your first clue?" I asked.

"The gleam in your eye when you came out of the kitchen, then the way you dragged me out of the house, and now the way you're driving."

"That's your first three clues. I only asked for one. But aside from that, what tipped you off?"

"Please, Gil, just tell me what you found out. Who'd you call?"

"Pop Miller."

"Did he say the sound was like the Time Machine?"

"Yeah, only not as loud."

"Further away?"

"Possibly, but it's more likely it was muffled by two factors — size and distance. It's obvious he couldn't have heard the Time Machine portals from there, so it had to be something different, only similar. Since it wasn't real loud, let's just say, for the sake of argument, it was something small. A small electrical device that crackles and pops —"

"Like when electricity jumps across an open space — like when you were going to touch Dave's sculpture."

"Exactly. From one pole to another. Like those big gizmos in science fiction movies, those machines the mad scientists have."

"Perhaps a small electrical device that generates some type of electric current or spark."

"A hand-held thing, operated inside the building. Close enough to be heard by someone, but not kept on long enough to make them too curious or give them a chance to pinpoint it. For that matter, it didn't need to be on longer than a few seconds, and whoever had it might not have known Miller was outside."

Sally nodded, trying to assimilate all our speculation and assemble it into a coherent picture.

"I'm not getting it," she admitted.

"A stun gun, Sally. One of those little personal protection devices. A few seconds of getting zapped with one of those can knock anyone out of commission for a few seconds, long enough to tie them up or drag them into a closet."

"Oh my," she said, her face clearly showing her alarm as the import of my theory registered. "You're saying Mrs. Potter was zapped with a stun gun after she came into her office?"

I nodded. "Looks probable."

"But who would do that?" Sally wondered. "And why? And where is she? Is she dead? What's going on?"

"I can't answer all those questions, Sally," I admitted, "although I have a few ideas."

"Jerry Opperman?"

"First and best suspect," I said. "And not only because I don't like him. It's his office, his secretary, and nobody on the planet would have a reason to do that to Mrs. Potter except someone about whom she had a lot of information — maybe even some information she wasn't supposed to have."

"She knew something he didn't want her to know."

"Makes sense. Whatever it is, it's got to be connected with the dismissal of Michelle Yokoyama. It's no coincidence the two events occurred the same week. First he zaps Potter for what she knows, then — wait a minute!" I pounded the steering wheel. "Of course. That has to be it."

"What?"

"That's why she wanted to see me. She was going to tell me some damaging piece

of information about Opperman. He overheard her, took care of her before I got
there —"

"He just happened to have a stun gun
lying around?"

"Maybe. Some people get them for protection, like they do with tear gas. And
maybe he was planning something anyway.
And maybe the stun gun was hers. She's an
old lady, remember? She rides the buses."

"But didn't Jerry come in right after you
left, according to Mr. Miller?"

"Yeah. So what? There's obviously some
other way in and out of that place. Old man
Golden was big on that, you know."

"I wonder what she knew, if that's the
case," Sally mused. "And what did it have
to do with Michelle? Michelle wasn't a threat
to Jerry. She was happy where she was, even
before she made senior vice president." Sally
stared absentmindedly out the window at the
passing scenery.

"People like Jerry see a threat in anybody
smarter or more talented than themselves.
Or better liked. Doesn't matter what Michelle thought — Jerry perceived her as a
threat. So something's going on, Potter
found out about it and was about to blow
the whistle, and Jerry silenced her, then got
rid of his competition as he perceived it." I

glanced at Sally as I finished and noticed the anxiety that had crawled over her face. I reviewed what I'd just said, then added, "I don't mean he silenced her in the permanent sense, just that he kept her from exposing him, from telling me about him. That's how I read it, at least. I might be completely wrong."

Sally was quiet as an unexpected rain began to splatter the windshield. I turned the wipers on as it increased and continued my way through town.

"Where are we going?" Sally asked after a while. "When we left Mr. Whelan's, you seemed in a hurry."

"I still am." I turned into a driveway. "We're here."

"Yes, I see that. Why?"

I pulled up to the receiving gate guard booth and stopped to talk to the security officer.

"Hi, Ernie. We'll just be a second. Have to go in and check something." I took off before he could protest and drove straight to the administration office, parking in Jerry Opperman's private space.

"Gil, what are you doing?"

"We, Sally, what are *we* doing?" I got out of the car.

"Okay, what are *we* doing?" She stepped

out of the car somewhat hesitantly and followed me to the door. I slipped in my security master key and with a furtive, melodramatic glance in both directions unlocked the door and pushed it slowly open. It was dark inside, so I retreated to the BMW and retrieved a flashlight from the trunk. We went inside, and I shut the door, locking it behind us.

"The scene of the crime, is that it?" Sally asked.

"Best place to start."

I looked across the room with the flashlight, then clicked it off and let the near-darkness return. Sally moved closer to me.

"What's going on, Gil?" she asked in a whisper, as though being in a dark place necessitated silence as well as cautious movement.

"Remember how when we were at Dave's, he said Jerry was hiding in his office last week, taking food back there to eat, and lots of it. I think it wasn't for him, and he wasn't hiding in his office."

"What then?"

"Zapping Potter was a spur of the moment thing. He overheard her call for me, realized she knew something, and grabbed the stun gun to shut her up. But he didn't kill her, didn't want to. He stuck her someplace and has been feeding her. He's trying to figure out what to do. The shake-up might be just a diversion, although I doubt if that's all it is. Jerry's an opportunist, and getting rid of Michelle was something he couldn't do before — before Mrs. Potter was out of the picture. That has to be it."

"That's pretty wild speculation," Sally said. "Wait a second. This is all so surreal. You're suggesting that the president of an amusement park is keeping his secretary hostage because she found out he was planning something illegal or immoral, and then he fired his senior vice president because he's afraid of her and couldn't do it before because his secretary, now his hostage, wouldn't let him."

She was right — it sounded stupid. Caught up in the excitement of discovery, the game afoot, had I lost touch with reality? Was I making a mountain out of a molehill — a crime out of an unexplained circumstance? Maybe I'd been caught up in investigating things so long, I just naturally assumed everything I couldn't explain was because criminal activity was involved.

The Moriarty syndrome, I called it. Sherlock Holmes was sure his nemesis, Professor Moriarty, was at the bottom of every crime in Victorian London, no matter how insignificant. Was I obsessing like my hero?

A footstep on the porch precluded an answer to Sally, and as she tossed a frantic look my way, I put my finger to my lips and pointed to the hallway. She immediately darted around the corner and disappeared, and I dove under Mrs. Potter's desk just as a key was inserted into the lock, the door swung open, and light flooded the room.

THIRTEEN

Somewhere in the world birds were chirping, water tumbled over rocks, and wind blew lightly through the evergreens. Somewhere on our peaceful planet squirrels ate acorns, fish broke the still surface of a small mountain lake, and smoke curled from the chimney of an isolated mountain cabin.

But that was last week and a zillion miles away. Right now I was crouching under a desk — not for the first time in my illustrious career as a security officer. Only this time I wondered why I was doing it. Why hide? So I was in Mrs. Potter's office. Big deal. Even if this was Opperman walking in, I had nothing to fear. I could bamboozle him. After all, it's not like I was committing a crime or anything.

And yet, even while thinking these thoughts, berating myself for cowering under a desk, I cowered under the desk, holding my breath and hoping whoever it was wouldn't linger. Or find me.

I heard the creaking of leather and the grainy squawking of a two-way radio and the jingle of keys.

A security officer, doing his rounds.

He walked past the desk and into the hall-way, jiggled the knob of Jerry's office door, then did the same to every other door in the hallway.

The presence of my car outside apparently didn't concern the officer. It was a common enough occurrence for cars to be parked here and there in the backstage area. He returned to Mrs. Potter's desk and stopped beside it, dropping some papers, probably interoffice memos, then playing with something on the desk. I could see the toes of his unshined black leather tennis shoes, mere inches from my face, but was transfixed by something else, something on the carpet itself.

In a moment he'd gone, clicking off the light and locking us in. I waited a little longer just to make sure he didn't double back for some reason, then turned on my flashlight and ran my fingers over the carpet fibers.

The little colored specks jumped as my hand brushed over them.

"Gil?" Sally called tentatively from her hiding place.

"It's okay, Sally. Come on out."

I extricated myself from my lair and was regaining my legs as Sally emerged, her hair disheveled and a look of fear on her face.

"Who was it?" she asked, her voice hoarse.

"Security officer," I told her. "Routine patrol. He probably won't return for a while, if at all. I need to use the telephone."

"Why don't we just get out of here?" Sally suggested. "I'm beginning to feel real funny about this. Don't get me wrong, it's not that I don't trust your judgment, but —"

"That's okay, I was beginning to have my own doubts. But before we go, there's something I need to do."

I grabbed the receiver.

"No!" Sally called. "The switchboard will know there's someone in here. It's the way the phone system is designed. Jerry's office has a private line. Use that."

"Thanks." I replaced the receiver and went to Jerry's door, stuck my key in, turned it slowly, and went inside, flipping on the light, which wouldn't be visible from outside. It was all I could do not to stand in the middle of his office and turn slowly, gawking at all the junk on his shelves — trinkets and pictures and memorabilia. I also hoped — unrealistically, perhaps — that I'd see a stun gun sitting out in plain view. Naturally, I didn't. The office was kind of cool, actually. Lots of neat stuff. I did notice a complete absence of anything related to the park mascot, Everett the Dinosaur, however. That hadn't been his idea. How he must hate the little creature.

What a delicious thought — Jerry Opperman having to see him and hear about him constantly, every time he set foot on the property. No wonder he locked himself in the office all the time. Every foray into the amusement park was a reminder that he was not the all-pervasive influence he thought himself to be.

He was the president, yes, but not the creative mastermind. No Walt Disney, this Jerry Opperman. It must've been truly painful for him. Heh heh.

But I didn't have time for that now. I grabbed for the phone on his desk — but there wasn't one. There were models — a large train engine, a motorcycle, a jukebox, a Ferrari. Wait a minute — these were all phones! I lifted them all until finally one of the many models gave out a dial tone.

I dialed Theo at home.

"Good evening, buddy," I said when he answered.

"Who is this?" He sounded tired.

"You know who," I assured. "How'd the investigation go?"

"Not too good, Gil. You know these gangs. They won't tell us anything. They'll take care of it themselves. It's getting real old."

"You need to get some sleep."

"I was trying to, but some jerk keeps calling. What do you want?"

"Two things. One, we missed you at church today. Saw Michelle, had a nice conversation."

"Thanks. I wanted to go. Maybe I'll make it next week. What's number two?"

"Did Sheriff Thomas ever call you? You know, that homicide we solved for him?"

"We hardly solved it. And no, he hasn't phoned. I doubt he will. Why?"

"Oh, just curious. Well, thanks. I'll let you get to bed now. I'll talk to you later when you're not so crabby." I hurried to hang up before he could answer, then punched in another number, reading it from a card in my wallet.

"Sheriff's Department, Deputy Walton."

"Evening, Deputy. This is Gil Beckman. Does Sheriff Thomas happen to be in?"

"Mr. Beckman? You're the guy that rescued those folks in the crash, right? I heard your name tossed around. No, sir, he's home. Can I give him a message, maybe have him call you back?"

"I'm not at a phone he can call in on, but maybe you can help me."

"I'll try."

"Your homicide from last week, the real estate lady?"

"I think I remember it," he said. "We have

one every fifteen years or so — it's hard to keep them separate."

"Did you catch anyone yet?"

"As a matter of fact, Mr. Beckman, we did. Brought him in this afternoon. Sheriff told me they took the tips you gave him and canvassed the area. Found two homes with small white dogs, several with philodendrons on the porch, four or five with gold carpet, even one with a philodendron and gold carpet — but only one house in the whole area with all three. A young guy lived there with his mother. There was a hammer in the garage with the victim's blood on it. He confessed and everything."

"That's good news!" I winked at Sally. "Tell me, Deputy Walton, did they come up with the source for those little colored specks in the soles of her shoes?"

"As a matter of fact, they did. It's so obvious, I don't know why we didn't figure it out sooner. Those are paint chips and glass fragments from colored Christmas lights, the kind people string around the eaves of their houses. The suspect had put his lights up a few weeks ago, said he dropped a few on the driveway. He swept the pieces up but not too good. Most of the debris stayed in the cracks in the driveway."

I was stunned, and as the wheels turned

in my head, I looked slowly at Sally.

"What is it?" she whispered, perplexed.

"Mr. Beckman, you there?"

"Yes, yes, I'm here. You've been very helpful, Deputy. I'm glad you caught the man. Thanks."

"Do you still want to talk to the sheriff?"

"No. You've answered my questions. Thanks."

"See you later." He hung up.

I did the same and turned to look through Jerry's open door and down the long hall, to the door at the end with two locks.

"What was that all about?" Sally asked. I hadn't told her about the homicide up in the mountains. I'd forgotten about it with all the goings-on down here.

"She's in there," I told her, pointing at the door marked SUPPLIES, the door that actually gave access to a large, formerly secret warehouse, one that Sally and I had discovered several months before while investigating another caper.

"How do you know that?" she asked.

"Come here." I exited Jerry's office, leaving the door open, and showed her the colored specks on the carpet by Mrs. Potter's desk. I explained they were just like those found in the homicide in the mountains, and I'd just found out what they were.

"Even if they are the same thing, how does that mean Mrs. Potter's in there?"

"I'll lay odds this place has some little colored lights somewhere in that room. You remember what it looked like — all that stuff everywhere." I bent over and walked around, looking for more specks, and my diligence was rewarded. There were plenty of specks, leading from the warehouse door to Jerry's office, most of them near the wall where the vacuum wouldn't reach.

"But that room's probably empty now, Gil. Or close to it."

I gaped up at Sally. "Huh?"

"Gil, don't you remember? They put it all in the new museum."

"When?"

"Last week — oh, that's right, you were gone."

"How'd they get it all out?"

"Turns out there were large doors down the far wall, and Mr. Golden had built a false wall outside them to beautify it. They took it down, pulled the stuff out, and put it back up."

I was crestfallen, my theory beginning to evaporate. And yet, someone had gone in there through this door, repeatedly. And recently. I crawled into Mrs. Potter's office and under her desk.

"Oh, really, Gil, there's no need to hide. It's not you —"

"I'm not hiding, Sally. I'm getting the key," I explained, reminding Sally about the key Mrs. Potter kept on a small hook in the well of the desk. I stuck my head out. "But it's not here."

"Gone?" Sally asked. "Why would it be gone?"

I stood up and sighed. "So no one can go in, of course. Are there any other rooms around here that no one goes in?"

"I don't think so —"

"Wait a minute. What was it Pop Miller said when he was rambling on about Golden? The two of them were playing cards and Mrs. Potter —"

"She came in to see them."

"No, she came *down* to see them. I distinctly recall he said 'down.' Obviously, he was talking about here since Mrs. Potter was involved. But why would he say 'down' unless . . ."

"Call him," Sally urged. "Don't guess — find out exactly what he meant."

"Good idea." I still had his number, so I went back into Jerry's office and dialed it. Unfortunately, all I got was a message machine. The old guy was probably already in bed.

I hung up the train thoughtfully. "Didn't this building used to be part of Golden's manufacturing plant?"

"Yes. The main building, in fact."

"And he converted it during the war for some secret government project?"

"Yes."

"Sally . . ." I grabbed her arms firmly and held her, looking directly into her eyes. "If you were eccentric Mr. Golden, doing secret stuff for the government on the West Coast, with a constant fear of Japanese attack . . . ?"

The color drained from her face. "Oh my, Gil."

"Yes," I said. "A bunker. Just like Saddam Hussein." I looked toward the door, sized it up, then let go of Sally and ran full bore toward the door, launching myself into it shoulder first as hard as I could.

There was a loud, hollow crack as I nailed it with my left shoulder, but it didn't open, and I bounced back, landing in a heap on the floor. But I wasn't finished. I regained my legs, backed up, and tried again. This time I felt something give as a tearing pain shot through my shoulder.

"Please, Gil, stop," Sally begged. "You're going to hurt yourself."

"Nonsense," I told her. "I already did." I

held my left arm in place with my right hand to isolate the shoulder and backed off, turning to face Sally as she stood in Jerry's doorway, my face expressing my desperation, hers her fear.

"Get some help," Sally exhorted.

I saw beyond her into the office. "Good idea." I walked past her and went behind Jerry's desk, but instead of sitting down in his chair to use the phone — his famous, high-dollar, heated, vibramassage, all-leather executive chair with power adjust and lumbar support — I got behind the grotesque thing and, with a shout for Sally to get out of the way, pushed it out of the office and down the hall as fast as I could go.

I hit the door, and it exploded inward, the dead bolts holding but the wood splitting vertically, as we — the chair and I — went down in a heap on the concrete. Fire ignited in my upper body as I tumbled, but when I came to rest, I was still conscious and quickly started picking myself up.

Sally had followed me down the hall, protesting, and helped me up, criticizing me nonstop for my actions. I just smiled. I had not only conquered the door — I had taken care of Opperman's goofy chair, that symbol of his vanity and excess.

I recovered my flashlight and found the

light switch, flipping the one closest to the door. Nothing happened, so I put it back down and tried the next one, and three low-watt bare bulbs came on overhead, barely illuminating the cavernous room. But it was enough to see that it was practically empty.

Gone were the boxes and the model-T Ford and the Ark of the Covenant or whatever else had been in here.

"We're in big trouble," Sally said, her voice betraying her genuine fear.

I didn't answer but swept the flashlight beam around the room, curious, searching, hoping . . .

Mrs. Potter wasn't here, although that alone did not particularly bother or surprise me. She was somewhere below. But how did she get there? Where was the access?

I was firmly convinced that Golden had built himself a bomb shelter below ground, accessible from his manufacturing plant. It made sense, considering the nature of the work they did, and he may well have decided to maintain it after the war, while the amusement park was being built. It would be a handy apartment for him.

In fact, it had long been rumored that Golden often worked late, so it made sense that he had a place to sleep and a place he could retreat to during the day when things got hectic. Certainly Mrs. Potter knew about it, and apparently some of his cronies did also. I could picture him down there, smoking his cigars and playing cards with Pop Miller and drinking tea. One could even imagine without too big a stretch the other uses that such a hideaway could be put to. Not by Mr. Golden, of course, but by someone else.

When he died and the resulting owners' group sprang up from the local business community — Golden had no heirs — they would certainly pick someone to run the place while they reserved for themselves all the major financial decisions. And to that someone Mrs. Potter might entrust the secret hideaway so he could enjoy it as Golden had — kind of a perk. If she liked him, that is.

"Ah ha!" I shouted, my exclamation echoing in the cavern.

"What?" Sally responded, coming over to me. She had stayed by the door, more cautious than afraid. But now she walked over carefully to see what I'd found.

"See here?"

I pointed the light onto a bunch of boxes full of what appeared to be trash. One of them contained many tangled strings of ancient Christmas lights. The floor was littered with the debris of broken bulbs.

"Okay," she said. "You're right so far." She actually didn't sound too relieved. "But where is Mrs. Potter? Look around, Gil. This is a big empty room."

"Somewhere there has to be a passage down to some underground rooms." I explained my theory and in doing so convinced myself even more of its likelihood. "Seriously, Sally, it fits. Mrs. Potter comes in but doesn't leave. No trace of her is found. Jerry brings large amounts of food back here to the office. It's obvious someone has been in and out of this storeroom."

"But I don't understand why he'd do it."

"Frankly, Sally, I don't care why at this moment. Whatever she knew, it would have to be real damaging to him, so damaging that he had to take drastic steps to keep her from telling. It has to be more than just to keep his job. He's on shaky ground anyway. He might even have figured out a way to gain some kind of controlling interest so he couldn't be fired."

"Like buying stock?"

"Something like that, but I doubt he could afford it."

"You don't think it involved Michelle?" Sally ventured.

"Anything's possible these days, but I

don't think so. How would it involve her?"

Sally didn't know, and we fell silent as we stared around the room. My eyes lit on the damaged chair and split door hanging crudely from hinges on one side, the rest of it, with dead bolts still extended, on the floor under the chair.

"Japanese," Sally said suddenly. "She's Japanese."

"Yeah? So?"

"And close to George Ozawa, the true heir to Hiromoto's empire. Why else would both of them be fired? George was just a landscaper."

I pressed my hand to my forehead. "That's it! Jerry was Eric Hiromoto's insider for accomplishing a hostile takeover or leveraged buyout or some scam like that. With Michelle around, and her being close to the Hiromotos, they might be found out. If she was part of it, there'd be no need to get rid of her. But apparently Mrs. Potter discovered the plot."

"That's what she was going to tell you," Sally suggested. "Who else could she trust that has the gumption to stand up and say something?"

"Or so little to lose?" I added. I closed my eyes and said quietly, "And I let her down."

"There's no time for self-pity," Sally said.

"Besides, it wasn't your fault. What's important now is that we find her — if she's still alive."

"She's still alive," I assured her. "If he'd been of a mind to kill her, he'd have done it right then. But the sad fact is, Sally, the longer he keeps her alive, the more desperate he'll become. Soon he's going to realize that he can't go on like this indefinitely, that he's got to end it. He can bring her up and confess and go to jail like a good little criminal, or he can kill her and dump her body somewhere. But *status quo* isn't an option for long. Of course, there's always the possibility that he's already made his decision . . ."

That didn't sit well with Sally, but it wasn't meant to.

"Then what are we waiting for?" she cried. "Let's find the way down!"

"Attagirl," I said proudly.

Seeing no obvious doors or other openings, we took to the walls, feeling, probing, trying to find the passage, inspecting them carefully. Why Golden would have hidden the access to his hideaway I couldn't guess, but perhaps he was a little like people in novels who build mystery houses where seemingly incongruous things like doors that open onto brick walls, stairways to the ceiling, and windows in the floor are a puzzle to us, without any reason behind them, yet make absolute sense to them. The door opening onto a block wall would one day have entered a new room, but the room was never built. The stairway used to go to another floor, but it burned and was never reconstructed. The window in the floor allowed one to keep an eye on a thieving kitchen staff.

Whatever his reasons, Golden had apparently not left the access to his hideaway readily visible. If it existed at all.

We examined the walls, searching for joints and rapping on them, listening for that hollow sound that would indicate a passage. But our efforts were fruitless. The pain in my shoulder was not subsiding, and I knew I'd need to get it looked at soon or forever suffer the consequences.

I couldn't imagine being wrong about this. But then, I couldn't imagine being wrong about anything. All the clues fit; all the clues pointed at a secret room down there somewhere.

So why couldn't we find it?

I finally sat down on a rectangle of concrete, four feet by three feet, maybe three feet high, in the center of the room, obviously a footing for some large piece of machinery from the manufacturing plant days.

Four large bolts had been sticking up on the top from the four corners to anchor something, but with the removal of the machinery they had been cut off flush with the surface so they wouldn't be a danger. Sally came over to me and sat on my good side, snuggled against my shoulder, and put her arms around me.

I'd be lying if I said I didn't enjoy it, but I had the feeling it was born partly of despair over not being able to locate Mrs. Potter and partly out of sympathy for me, not because of my injury, which I'm sure she chalked up to my headstrong, impulsive nature, but because it was evident I'd been wrong. There was no hideaway bunker below us, Mrs. Potter wasn't down there, and there was no sinister plot by Jerry Opperman.

My imagination had run amok this time.

FOURTEEN

I closed my eyes. I was tired and in pain, but it was beginning to subside, and I could raise my arm a little. Maybe the shoulder wasn't broken, just bruised and tender. I was more depressed than anything.

"Come on, Gil," Sally said tenderly, her tone betraying the defeat we both felt. I looked into her soft, moist eyes, her skin a warm yellow in the light of the incandescent bulbs high overhead. "We were wrong. Let's get that arm taken care of."

"I'm okay," I told her. To leave was to admit defeat. I'd rather stay, at least until Jerry found me and saw what I'd done to his chair. The look on his face would be worth whatever my punishment would be. Almost.

"You go on," I said. "I'll wait until you leave, then call Sgt. Howard over so I can show him what I did. No need you getting caught up in my fiasco."

She hesitated but knew I was right. She knew I couldn't leave without 'fessing up, even if it meant getting arrested.

Of course, I knew the park wouldn't prosecute — they never do. But I was afraid this

238

meant the end of us, me and her. I'd run headlong into a block wall, and there was no turning back. If she was smart, she'd forget me.

Anger welled up inside me — anger at myself — and I slammed my metal flashlight impetuously on the edge of the concrete footing we sat on. I fully expected the flashlight to break or at least dent, but I didn't care. I had adrenaline surging through me, and I needed an outlet. So I was a little surprised when the flashlight not only didn't break, but a large chunk of the concrete broke off and fell to the floor.

"Gil, be careful," Sally chastised.

But I didn't answer. I was looking at the break, amazed. The exposed surface was pure white and mostly smooth, not gray and rough. I hit it again. It broke some more, and more white material was exposed, along with some thin wire. Chicken wire. Leaning over for a closer look, I dug at the material with my fingernail.

"Gil, what is it? What's the matter?"

"Plaster!" I said excitedly.

"What?" Sally didn't understand the significance.

"This isn't concrete — it's plaster!" I jumped up, pulling Sally off the block. I grabbed the edge with both hands and pushed, but it didn't move. Then I changed my position and pushed a different direction. Still nothing. I kicked it, still without success.

I stood back and examined it for a second, then shouted, "Open sesame!" Of course, nothing happened, and Sally looked at me like I'd just announced I was the Pope.

I grinned at her sheepishly. "You never know," I explained.

"What are you trying to do?"

"This isn't what it appears," I explained. "It's made of plaster-of-paris and wire, and it's probably hollow. It's relatively light." Still nothing registered on her face. "It's light enough to be moved."

"Then why isn't it moving?"

"I don't know." I kicked it out of frustration just as I said the word *know,* aiming at the nearest corner.

Success! It shifted — ever so slightly, but it definitely moved.

Sally watched, enraptured. "Maybe it swivels."

I gave her that look all men give women when they're trying to interfere in something that's entirely man's domain and they couldn't possibly know what they're talking about. So she bent over, lifted up slightly on the corner, and shoved it sideways. The corner dislodged from a slight depression in the floor, and the whole block pivoted quietly away, connected only at one corner, exposing a large hole in the floor.

"You were right," Sally said judiciously, and I didn't correct her.

I shone my light down into the abyss with much the same feeling the early miners must have had when their pick loosened a chunk of quartz and revealed a thick vein of gold.

There was a steep, wooden staircase leading down from the narrow opening to a hallway below. From my position I couldn't see anything else. Sally took my arm.

"Gil . . ." she breathed.

"Let's not waste any more time," I said. "You coming?"

"Down there?"

"Of course. We've come this far. I'm not stopping now!"

She gulped audibly. "Okay. L-let's go."

I went first, holding the flashlight in one hand and Sally's hand in the other. The stairs were walled on both sides. Sally put her free hand on the wall to steady herself. I looked at her and pursed my lips to warn her to be as quiet as possible. There was no telling what was down there.

As I neared the bottom, my light revealed a long hallway, no wider than the staircase, stretching away from the foot of the stairs. The walls, floor, and ceiling were all lined with flat stones. There were light fixtures attached to the ceiling, the wiring encased in conduit, but there was no visible switch. Sally gripped my hand tightly.

Without comment, I advanced slowly down the passage, keeping my light low. Our feet scuffed the stones, but I could imagine the hollow click and resulting echo we would have made had we been wearing hard-soled shoes. This was an eerie place. That it was underneath a theme park made it all the more strange.

"What do you make of this?" I whispered to Sally without taking my eyes off the passage ahead.

"I-I don't know."

"Let's see what's around this corner."

The passage made a sharp right turn, then continued in a slow arc to the right, limiting our view to about ten feet. But on the left side, just within view, was an opening. Sally saw it also and tightened her grip on my hand.

I continued forward, not heedless of the possible dangers around the corner, just unconcerned with them. This was taking too long, and after all, what's the worst thing that could happen? We'd meet up with Jerry.

Big deal. I did that all the time.

Sally began to breathe heavily and gripped my arm with both hands.

"Relax," I told her. "You watch too many scary movies. There's nothing down here — except Mrs. Potter, hopefully. No monsters, no crazed gunmen, no vampires, not even any bats."

"If you say so," Sally acquiesced.

"Maybe just some rats and lots of gushy, yucky insects."

When she didn't respond, I stopped and glanced back at her. Sally's silent reproach bored a hole through my forehead. Then she put words to her thoughts.

"You're such a jerk."

"Thank you, I know you mean that in a positive way. Wait here."

She let go of me, and I stepped toward the opening, which was doorway-sized but without a door, just an arched portal. I shone the light through first, then followed with my right eyeball, then my whole head.

"Oh no," I groaned under my breath.

"What is it?" Sally whispered hoarsely.

"Another passage."

"What kind of place is this?"

"Golden's labyrinth."

"Labyrinth?"

"Maze. We're rats in a maze, Sally."

243

"Why would Golden build a labyrinth?"

"I don't know. We could ask that guy down there, but I doubt skeletons talk."

"What?" Sally shouted and started to run down the passage. I caught her hand, held on, and began laughing.

"It's okay, Sally. I'm kidding. There's nothing down there but Golden's humidor."

"Gilbert Beckman, you dirty, rotten . . ." She checked herself, then asked, "Humidor?"

"Yeah. Remember Pop Miller saying Golden didn't need one? That's because the temperature and moisture down here was good enough for it. There's a little cubbyhole in there, with shelves and some old cigar boxes lying around."

"Maybe we should mark our trail anyway," Sally suggested. "Just in case this does have some other passageways."

"Okay. Break out the bread."

"Uh . . ."

"No bread? Roll of string maybe?"

"Well, I —"

"How about your sweater? You could unravel it."

"Oh, you'd like that."

I grinned. "Keep your sweater on, dear. We'll be okay. Come on."

We kept going, and the passage continued

to curve, first right, then left, until I wasn't sure what direction we were headed. I also had no idea how far we'd traveled, but I didn't think it was as far as it seemed.

"I'm getting claustrophobic," Sally said.

"It can't be much farther," I said. "Doesn't make sense for him to build a bunker that would take so long to get to that he wouldn't make it in time. It's probably not directly underneath the plant either. That wouldn't make sense."

Suddenly we were there. A door. Straight ahead, finally. At the end of the passage . . . No, not the end. On the far side of another passage crossing at a right angle, like a capital *T*. That had to be the bunker apartment. If she was down here at all, she'd be behind that door.

"Sally, wait here." I crept ahead to size up the situation. I didn't want to bust in if I didn't have to, for several reasons, one of them painfully obvious. In addition, I didn't know if Opperman was inside, although at this hour I doubted it. Nor did I want to harm Mrs. Potter if she was standing too close to the door. I suppose I could have called to her, but what was the fun in that?

The hallway was clear, and there were no other doors visible. The perpendicular passage to my left receded only about ten feet to a dead end. To my right, there was a sharp left turn about the same distance away. I turned to Sally and put my finger to my lips, then moved quickly down the tunnel to the right.

I peered cautiously around the corner, flashlight first, dismayed to see the passage continue beyond my light's beam. There was one notable difference between this passage and the rest — the stones lining the walls, floor, and ceiling stopped, giving way to wood shoring like a mine, and it was narrow and rough-hewn. It looked to be an escape tunnel or perhaps a secondary entrance.

I'd long since lost my sense of direction and wondered where this new tunnel ended up. This might explain how Jerry was able to leave the park undetected. Maybe it came up somewhere outside.

I retreated to Sally's position and told her what I'd found.

"I want to follow it," I said.

"Mrs. Potter . . ." she reminded me, glancing at the door with concern, almost fear, in her eyes.

She was right. If Mrs. Potter was down here, she'd be in that room. Moving Sally aside, I prepared myself to once again use my body as a battering ram and assault the door. I wasn't looking forward to it, but it was all I had to work with. I hoped the door wasn't as sturdy as the other one, or that I'd at least get knocked unconscious so the pain wouldn't be so bad. Maybe I should use the other shoulder.

Sally put her hand on my arm. "What are you doing, Gil?"

"I'm going to knock it down."

She rolled her eyes heavenward. "Hold on one second, please." She walked to the door before I could stop her and softly called, "Mrs. Potter? Elizabeth! Are you in there? It's me, Sally, and Gil's here too."

I cringed. Sally paused and listened, but there was no response. As she put her hand on the knob I thought, *Don't be silly. It won't be unlocked. How would they keep her inside?*

Sally tried it, and the knob turned easily.

FIFTEEN

Sally pushed the door open and stepped aside, giving me a faint smile in the dim glow of my flashlight.

I grinned sheepishly. Okay, I was wrong. So sue me.

Stepping forward cautiously, I gripped my flashlight like a club just in case.

I entered a well-appointed — albeit musty-smelling — apartment, just like any other you might see except this one had low ceilings and no windows. This first room was the living room, with a sofa, easy chair, coffee table, lamps . . .

I clicked one on, and light flooded the room. A second switch by the door activated the lights down the center of the passageway ceiling, the way we'd just come. There was a bookcase filled with old tomes, the most recent no less than a decade old, a braided rug on the floor, even a small dusty piano in the corner. The walls were covered with paintings, most of them originals.

But there was no Mrs. Potter.

Off to one side was a doorway to what proved to be a bathroom. Toiletries — ladies' toiletries — were arranged neatly on a small shelf. Small drops of water stood in the tiny sink. The porcelain throne was clean, both lids down.

"She's been here," I concluded to Sally.

We retreated from the bathroom to another room on the far side of the living room, which we expected to be the bedroom. We were correct. Although neat, it had obviously been recently used. But it too did not contain Mrs. Potter.

"Somebody's been sleeping in my bed," I joked.

"Better not have been Goldilocks," Sally said under her breath.

There were no other rooms — no kitchen, no second bedroom, no large closet. This was just a small hideaway with a hot plate and a bar-sized refrigerator next to the bed. I noticed the place was vented to the outside, both to draw out the bad air and bring in the good. I made a mental note to find the outside pipes for the vents sometime. We stood with our backs to the door, staring at the room in silence as if by doing so we could make our friend appear. We both knew — I perhaps more than Sally — that Mrs. Potter's being moved was not a good sign. There'd be no reason for that except to prevent her being found or because she was injured, ill, or dead.

"Now what?" Sally asked.

"We keep looking," I said. "There's more tunnel beyond here."

A sudden noise behind us spun me around instinctively, and I raised the flashlight to strike. But before I could, I saw the sneering face of Jerry Opperman and heard the crackling from the stun gun in his hand.

I had nowhere to back up, so I brought the flashlight down to strike his wrist. But he made contact on my abdomen before I connected, and the voltage surged through me. I remember seeing stars and feeling all my muscles twitch, my hair tingle, and my teeth ache. I also have a vague recollection of Sally raking the sole of her shoe down Opperman's shin while he cried out, and the juice stopped flowing, but I was already on my way down.

Then there was a bright light moving toward me, or was I drifting toward it? I was floating, arms and legs hanging limp. I wondered, *Is this it? Am I on my way to heaven?*

A voice, soft and sweet, spoke my name. An angel had come to guide me to my eternal home, my mansion on Gold Street. The light got brighter and brighter —

Suddenly it blinked out, and all was darkness. *Oh no, how could this be? Was it all those puns, or perhaps my chronic cynicism? How could I —*

"Gil! Wake up! Are you okay? It's me — Sally."

I forced one eye open, and as it dilated I could make out her face, hovering just above me. My eyelids twitched, and my tongue tasted like tinfoil.

"Sally?"

She still held the flashlight above me, though it was now off, and as I understood, I groaned and closed my eyes. Whew! It wasn't my time yet! Don't get me wrong. It's not that I didn't want to go to heaven right then. It's just that I wanted to solve this little mystery first.

She helped me up and sat me on the edge of the bed. Jerry Opperman hunkered in the corner on the floor, nursing a painful shin, the very picture of a broken, beaten man. Was he actually crying?

In her other hand Sally held the stun gun. True to form, Opperman had caved in at the least resistance.

I stood on shaky legs and hobbled over to him.

"Take that!" I told him. "Now, where is she, Jerry?" When he didn't answer, I asked Sally, "Did you try zapping it out of him?"

Jerry shot me a look of abject fear as Sally

251

told me, "Of course not."

"I really don't know," Jerry whimpered.

"Give me a break, Jerry," I said harshly. "Here we all are, in this underground bunker apartment where she's obviously been kept for a week. You sneak up on us with the stun gun you used to get her down here, all because she found out about your scheme, and you expect us to believe you don't know where she is? Give me that thing!" I said to Sally as I reached for the stun gun.

She pulled her arm back out of my reach. "Listen to him, Gil. Please remember, you're a Christian."

"I don't need to be reminded. I'm not going to hurt him — just jump-start his memory."

"Please," Jerry said. "I swear, I don't know anything about it."

"Okay, this I gotta hear," I said, sitting down on the bed. Truth is, I wasn't quite up to snuff yet and needed the rest. "But it had better be good or you'll be shocked by what I'm going to do to you. You can expect to get a real charge out of it."

"Please, Gil, no more puns," Sally said.

"I'm just getting started."

"You promised."

"Huh? When?"

"A few minutes ago, before you came out

of it. I heard you."

"Okay, okay," Jerry interrupted. We'd gotten to him. But was it the threat or the puns? I'd never know.

"Listen, Beckman," Jerry began, getting my name right for probably the first time ever.

"You can call me *Mr.* Beckman."

"Mr. Beckman, I came in to get some papers for a meeting tomorrow. They were on Miss Schilling's — I mean, Mrs. Potter's desk. And I saw my office door open and my chair gone. Then I saw what had been done to the storeroom door with my chair, and the lights came on down here, so I came downstairs. I thought you were robbers or something." He paused, but though I waited for him to continue, he didn't.

"That's it?" I asked after about ten seconds.

"Yes. That's all there is to tell you. That's the whole truth."

"Why didn't you call 911 or security?"

"I didn't think of it."

"Oh, come on. A little common sense will . . . Oh, okay, Jerry, I'll buy that."

"I was mad about my chair," he said, his face contorting. "You broke my chair! You owe me —"

"You'll get the chair, all right," I said, "if

anything has happened to Mrs. Potter."

"But I'm telling you, I don't know where she is. I know about this bunker, yes. Of course I do. But I don't come down here much. I haven't been here for a good six months. And I don't know where Mrs. Potter is."

"And where did the stun gun come from? Tell me that, Mr. Opperman."

"It's mine. I keep it in my office for protection. I got a permit for it from Captain Fitzgerald."

"It was used on Mrs. Potter the day she disappeared. Someone heard it from outside the office. They just didn't know what it was."

"She was here?"

"Yes, Jerry, she was. She was kidnapped from inside her office, as if you didn't know."

Opperman shook his head. "I didn't know. I've done nothing wrong."

I turned to Sally. "Now can I zap him?"

"Let me. Then we'll call the police."

I rested my forearms on my thighs and spoke to Jerry, who manifested deep fear and confusion on his sweaty face. "Look, Jerry, we have it on good authority that you've been bringing cafeteria food into your office in large quantities all week. We figure it was for Mrs. Potter."

He looked up sharply. "That's not true! I've done no such thing."

"We have a reliable witness, Jerry."

"He's lying!"

"Jerry, that's absurd. No one else knows about this bunker except you and Mrs. Potter."

As Jerry thought for a second, his forehead creased severely, then relaxed as he engaged our eyes.

"Dave Whelan knows about it. He knew about the stun gun too. I showed it to him the day I got it. Was he your reliable witness?"

No sooner did he say that than something clicked in my brain — and clicked hard. I rolled the whole thing around in my mind from every angle. It all fit.

"Look, Jerry, I'm going to tell you something. You listen, and you listen good." I stood up to add height intimidation to my finger-pointing. "Return to your office and call security. Have them hurry over to — wait, where does this passage go?" I pointed in the direction of the rough-hewn tunnel.

"Go?"

"How did Dave get down here to take care of her?"

He thought a minute. "I don't know where

the tunnel goes. I never went down it. It doesn't even look safe to me."

"Okay. Have security spread out through the park, but put at least one guy with you, and have one come down here and follow the tunnel. Sally, call the cops. Then both of you stay put. If you leave your office, Jerry, I'll . . . I'm not fully convinced of your innocence. Not by a long shot. If you leave, I'll know you're just as guilty as Dave. Is that clear?"

For a second he looked like the old Jerry, ready to bombast me with spit-peppered threats and outrages. But his face relaxed, and his eyes locked on Sally. She was holding the stun gun in front of her as she casually pressed the button. Little blue lightning bolts crackled between the electrodes.

"You're the boss," he said. Whether it was directed to me, Sally, or the stun gun, I wasn't sure.

"Frankly, Jerry, you have more reason to fear Sally than me. I'd probably make you unconscious real fast. Sally here'll take her time. Go on now, and don't dawdle."

I stood up and leaned into Sal to give her a kiss. "You gonna be okay?"

"Oh, sure. He won't try anything. It'll only be a few minutes until security gets there anyway."

"Okay. I love you. Be careful."

Surprised at first, she quickly regained her composure. "I love you too. And I want you back in one piece." With our hands between us, she slipped me the stun gun. "I'll be fine," she whispered.

I winked, and Sally followed Opperman out the door with her hand in her pocket for show.

I waited until they disappeared from view, then clicked on my flashlight and went to the entrance to the rough tunnel. I took a breath, then stepped forward.

I had no idea where the tunnel and I were headed. Although it meandered, it seemed to be headed mostly in one particular direction. I figured it had to be going to the amusement park, since there wasn't much point in it going anywhere else.

The reason for this I could only guess, but it seemed logical to me that once Golden hit on the idea for the amusement park, a tunnel would make it easier to get from his office to the far corner in a relatively straight line, with no winding around the attractions, no fighting the crowds.

The tunnel reminded me of a gold mine's narrow, shallow-ceilinged arteries wandering through quartz mountains, following the vein of precious ore, complete with cool, constant-temperatured drifts and crosscuts. I was a kid again, exploring, searching for treasure, half-expecting to meet up with Tom and Huck and Injun Joe — uh, Native American Joe.

But where would the tunnel come up? What would have been Golden's terminus for his underground shortcut? Certainly not something public. An office perhaps? Or maybe inside a ride. But which office or which ride? It would help to know what was here when he dug it, but I had no idea. I'd just have to follow the tunnel and hope the cavalry could find me.

I checked my watch. The park would be open for another hour, and when I had last looked, there had still been a good crowd. Funny, I realized for the first time, I couldn't hear anything from above when I first came down into the stone-lined passage. But now a throbbing hum — the sum of all the sounds from the park, mostly the vibration of machinery — filled the tunnel, growing louder the further I traversed, until it reached its peak, indicating I was well under the amusement park.

It hadn't taken long, and less than five minutes into the journey I came to the first right-angle turn. There had been some gradual arcs, but those were probably incidental, the product of casual labor taking the easiest route.

I stopped at the corner. My breathing was sharp and deep, and the coolness of the dark tunnel clashed with the sweat dampening my shirt. I closed my eyes, clicked off the flashlight, and listened for any sound that might tell me I was close to my destination.

There was nothing special. A clanking sound, at regular intervals, metal on metal. One . . . two, three. One . . . two . . . three. More humming. I took the opportunity to ask God for guidance. No, not guidance. I knew where I was going, kind of. I needed strength, wisdom . . . and a new arm.

When this was over, I was going to consider a less exhausting profession. Like circus performer or jackhammer operator.

A door slammed shut. Did I hear that? It sounded close. I snapped on the flashlight and swung around the corner in a crouch. Up ahead, maybe twenty feet, I saw the end of the passage and a long, wooden staircase leading up to a door. My head dropped, and I slowly blew the air from my cheeks.

The problem was twofold. No, threefold. I didn't know who or what was on the other side, it was at the top of some stairs, so I couldn't get a running start, and my arm felt like it was pinned to my shoulder with a railroad spike. I gave the door a closer look.

Oops, a fourfold problem. It opened toward me.

Oh well, there was no turning back now. I was fresh out of options. I mounted the stairs, keeping the flashlight trained on the door and my other hand free. There were twenty steps or so to the landing, a rather long and bumpy fall ending on a somewhat rocky tunnel floor should I be forced to retreat against my will. I decided against letting that happen.

Then I noticed the door didn't have a knob, just a dead bolt, and it was only key-operated on the other side. This side had a lever. That made sense. Golden would've wanted to keep people out of the tunnel, not himself from going through from this side. I reached out and held the little lever between my thumb and first two fingers, applied slight, silent pressure, and turned it.

It moved. *Thank You, Lord.*

I backed down a couple of steps and crouched until I was nearly eye-level with the bottom of the door, then turned off my flashlight, throwing a blanket of complete darkness over myself. I reached out and grabbed the edge of the door with my fingertips and pulled it toward me slowly, expecting an excruciating and amplified metallic squeal from the hinges. But they were as silent as a nursing baby.

With the door now completely open, I aimed my light and snapped it on, flooding the room with high-intensity light.

SIXTEEN

It was a workroom of some sort. Okay, I had arrived at my destination. I crept forward on my hands and knees, checked right, then left inside the room as far as I could, and didn't see anyone. I went up on my feet in a crouch, then through the door, eyes darting, searching.

It was definitely a ride workroom. Greasy, with the telltale odor of lubricants and solvents and rubber and machinery and sweat. A diagram on the wall told me where I was. The park's oldest indoor ride, one of the first such rides in the country. It was only natural the tunnel would come here. It was Mr. Golden's *coup de grace* at the time, changing the park from a permanent carnival into a true theme park.

This was the Screaming Bobsled. Four lanes, each with its own Olympic-style sled (the screaming provided, apparently, by the riders) that carried up to four people, with all of the bobsleds released simultaneously, riding on rails around a twisting, gravity-powered track, over bumps, down steep inclines, around sweeping curves, at speeds up to fifty miles per hour, ending up where the ride began. Total ride time, about thirty seconds. Total wait time to get on the ride, about thirty minutes.

The ride hadn't always been the Screaming Bobsled. Or just plain-old Bobsled. It had gone through several transitions over the years that only required changes in the conveyances and the sparse decorations. Originally it had been the Steeplechase, and riders sat on goofy-looking horses that jumped over hedges and around water hazards, at a much slower speed of course. When they removed the ponies and replaced them with motorcycles, they took off the brakes. They learned quickly that the increased speed necessitated enclosed conveyances, so they changed the cycles to rockets, plunging the ride into near-dark conditions with stars projected onto the walls and ceiling.

Then the Winter Olympics came to the local mountains, and the idea for bobsleds was born. They were going to call it the Luge, but they found out after a survey that most people didn't know what a luge was. With the bobsleds came new decorations — lots of stark, white "snow banks," cheering crowd noises, victory music, whooshing sound effects, and blasts of frigid air at several places on the course.

Needless to say, it was a mite cold where

I stood. The ride operators all wore winter coats and hats to add to the illusion, although the mean temperature in the building probably never dipped below sixty. But come to think of it, this room was also connected to the cool tunnel, and the door to it had just been opened at least twice.

I couldn't have been more than a couple minutes behind them, if that. Where was he taking her? What did he possibly hope to gain now that we were on to him?

The thought processes of a crook's mind never cease to amaze me. Even intelligent people do really stupid, unexplainable things when they're on the verge of discovery — rash actions they might otherwise never even consider, that, if they stopped for a moment to reflect on it logically, they'd realize they could never get away with.

Yet here I was, pursuing a successful businessman who — for reasons I had yet to comprehend — had kidnapped an elderly woman and was now trying to escape with her in tow. A difficult task in perfect circumstances, Dave was trying to do it in a crowded theme park, with hundreds of potential witnesses once he came out into the open.

And where would he try to take her? He had to get away from the park, that was for sure. Sooner or later he'd head for his car, wherever it was. Once he was out of the amusement park and into the street, would he let her go? I wondered if he'd even thought about what he would do next.

I crossed the room carefully, wanting to hurry but not wanting to be reckless. Easing the door open slowly while pressing myself against the wall, I strained to look out onto the loading dock, twenty yards to the left and about eight feet above me, to see some sign from the throbbing masses of would-be Olympians that they were aware a man was keeping a woman against her will.

They gave no sign. Business as usual. Perhaps Whelan hadn't dragged Mrs. Potter out there yet.

A strained, muffled shout across the room startled me.

"Gi— !"

I spun my head back to see Mrs. Potter trying to emerge from behind a bank of lockers while Whelan clamped a hand over her face. He threw his other arm around her waist and yanked the squirming woman back to him. She didn't put up much of a fight. Her age and the week of confinement had taken its toll on her frail body.

The Dragon Lady's spirit wasn't dampened, but her fire had been quenched.

"Get back!" Whelan ordered me.

I held my hands up. "I'm not moving, Dave. And there's a wall behind me. I'm as back as I can get."

His eyes were wild, more from fear, I thought, than because he was deranged. A cornered rat, of sorts. A rat with a hostage. As far as I could tell, he had no weapon. His ace — his only card, in fact — was Mrs. Potter.

"Take it easy, Dave. What gives anyway?" I needed to buy time, hoping someone would follow me up the tunnel soon. Maybe I could even talk Whelan out of the situation. I didn't want to hurt him — I'd had to do enough of that lately — and I certainly didn't want anything to happen to Mrs. Potter.

"I had a feeling you'd figure it out," Dave said, breathing hard. "I don't know how, but apparently you did."

"I haven't," I said honestly.

"You're here."

"Okay," I admitted, "I knew Mrs. Potter had been taken somewhere, but —"

"I've got to give you credit."

"No," I told him, "I pay cash for everything."

"Huh?" His brows scrunched together briefly. In the midst of his crisis, dry sarcasm and irony were forms of humor that eluded

266

him. "No, I mean for finding her so quickly," he said.

"Lucky," I said. "Remind me later to tell you what happened. God provided a really neat clue —"

"Don't talk to me about God! And it's too bad you found us so quickly. That little trick put Mrs. Potter in jeopardy."

"The only one here putting her in jeopardy is you, pal. Let's get that straight." I slowly began to drop my arms, my injured shoulder threatening to reduce me to tears any second. But I couldn't let him know about the injury.

"Stay back, Beckman. I'm warning you."

"What're you gonna do, shoot me?" I mocked.

"In a way," he said, holding up a can of tear gas.

"Get that from Jerry's office too?"

"Actually it's mine. I took a course."

At least he didn't get it from Captain Fitzgerald. Permits are required in this state for private citizens to legally possess tear gas and stun guns.

"That was a good idea, Dave, getting something for your personal protection. You never know when you're going to get mugged or have to take a hostage."

"Unlike you, I'm not joking." He pointed

the can at me threateningly.

"Please don't," I said. "It's bad for my complexion." Remembering the stun gun in my pocket, I considered maneuvering him so I could get close enough to jerk it out quickly and zap him. But the canister of mace in his hand gave me pause. A person soaked with tear gas, then zapped with a stun gun can burst into flames. I knew it, and if Whelan had taken the course, he knew it too. I had to keep the stun gun a secret.

For now.

"So, what's this all about, Dave?" I asked. "I always like to know why I'm about to be sprayed with tear gas, don't you?"

"The Japanese," Mrs. Potter said weakly.

"Be quiet!" Dave snapped.

"You sold out?" I guessed. "Or did you sell out the park? Which was it?"

"Neither. Jerry did it. He was working with Eric Hiromoto to gain control of the corporation. I found out about it."

"Blackmail," I concluded. "Your silence in exchange for a high position. Like vice president."

Whelan laughed. "Not hardly, Beckman. I might as well tell you. You'll figure it out soon enough anyway. With Jerry on his way to Japan to run things there, the top spot here was wide open. Goodness knows I could do a better job running the park than Jerry."

"Who couldn't?" I asked with a shrug.

"But I earned it," Dave insisted. "I did a good job here."

"Why didn't you just wait?" I asked. "You'd've moved up eventually."

"Yeah, right. After how many years of Michelle Yokoyama —" He spat out her name. "— running the show?"

So that was it. The old "she's a woman" or "she's Japanese" objection from a white male. Or even "she's a Japanese woman." A double negative to some, especially those who are greedy, who have the I've-got-to-have-it-now attitude that permeates our society and who resent the progress of the Japanese since the war. That Michelle was American didn't faze people like that.

"So you two killed two birds with one stone, is that it?" I guessed. "Blackmailed Jerry and got rid of Michelle, all in one fell swoop." My arms were nearly down by now.

"Get those arms back up, Beckman!"

Shoot, he'd noticed. I complied but not quickly, trying not to wince as the pain increased tenfold with every inch I raised them. Kind of the Richter scale of pain.

"Enough stalling. I'm sure Mrs. Potter will tell you about it later, when I'm safely away.

Move around the room now, clockwise, real slow. Stay next to the wall. When you get to here, stop. You make any sudden moves, I spray her." He turned the can so the stream would go right into her face. "How much tear gas can an old lady take?"

"Depends on the old lady," I said. "The Dragon Lady puts that stuff on her corn flakes every morning."

I'm not positive, but I thought a smile flickered across Mrs. Potter's face.

"Fine," Dave said. "Then I'll just have to spray you both. Now get moving."

I didn't think Dave really wanted to do anything to her. Besides, if he sprayed her, he wouldn't be able to hold her up. And if he sprayed me, I'd just get real mad and probably take his head off. I'd been sprayed before, and it wasn't incapacitating. Irritating, yes. Incapacitating, no.

But at the same time I didn't want to press the issue. People like Whelan sometimes react with unexpected violence with their backs against the wall and all other options exhausted. I moved as ordered.

"Tell me something, Dave," I said respectfully as I inched my way around the edge of the room, Whelan and Mrs. Potter mimicking my progress along the opposite wall. "How'd you get here so quickly?"

"You left my house in a hurry," he said. "I knew you suspected something, though I don't know how you could have. Even if you were wrong, I couldn't take a chance. I followed you to the park, took the tunnel to the bunker, and brought her out. Another couple minutes, Gil, and I'd've been home free."

"So the story about Jerry taking her food — that wasn't true, was it?"

"You're the big detective. You figure it out."

"I'll take that as a compliment," I said. "You know it's hopeless, don't you? Why don't you give up now, Dave, before it gets any worse?"

"I can't do that, Gil."

People like Whelan always think they can somehow get away, disappear. Go to another state, take a new name, and everyone will forget about them. He apparently hadn't learned the futility of that from one of his own employees who'd tried it.

Very few even make it out of the building, much less the county or the state. But they all think they'll be the one to succeed where everyone else has failed. Just like every kid thinks he's the one who can play with matches and not get burned, or smoke dope and not get hooked.

The other guy made it for fifteen years and still got caught.

"Okay, Dave, I'm going to let you go. It's not like you killed anybody or anything like that. I'm sure if I can get Mrs. Potter to Billy Bob's Truck Stop pretty soon and stuff a few 18 Wheeler cheeseburgers down her, she'll be okay. Shoot, you're probably a hero. You stopped Jerry Opperman from selling out the park to the Japanese. Go on. Just leave her here."

"I can't do that, Gil. I don't trust you. You won't let me leave."

He was right, of course. But I figured if he let Mrs. Potter go, the best he'd have on me is a minute head start. Then I could give chase. If nothing else, I could phone security and alert all the officers and gate guards. Shoot, the cops were probably already here. People were looking for us. It was only a matter of time before we'd be found.

But he wasn't buying it. "No, she's fine right here with me."

"Why her, Dave?" I was still buying time. "What'd she do to figure in your plan in such a big way?"

"She found out. I don't know how, but she found out. I heard over the radio that morning she'd called you in to tell you, so I took care of her." Mrs. Potter was trying to tell me something with her eyes, but I couldn't read it. "Now that's enough talk," Dave added. "Get out of the way."

"I'm not in the way, Dave. I'm way over here, and you're by the door." This boy was really confused.

He looked around. "Oh, yeah." He opened the door and backed through it, pulling Mrs. Potter with him. Her gaze wasn't pleading or fearful; she seemed suddenly resigned to her fate. What she thought that might entail, I didn't know.

The door shut slowly on its automatic closer as Dave moved off with his hostage. As soon as he could no longer see me, I dropped my arms, the sudden motion sending an angry message to my brain's pain center, a much overworked area this past year. I bolted for the door and threw it open, preparing to duck should Dave be waiting for me.

But he was gone.

SEVENTEEN

Outside the door was a work area below the large rails that carried the bobsleds, and Whelan and Mrs. Potter were making their way toward another door on the far side, a door I believed led to the midway.

I stayed back until they were next to it, then started moving under the rails, which were elevated about six feet above the concrete so maintenance folk could work on the bobsleds standing up. I could run in a crouch without bumping my head. What I hadn't taken into account was the under-hanging superstructure built to accommo-date the wheel and brake assemblies and counterweights on the bottoms of the bob-sleds. I also didn't realize this wasn't a ser-vice area but the live track. At least until I heard the roar of the oncoming sleds as they rounded the turn and roared right at me.

I dropped to the concrete hard, losing my flashlight, as the bobsleds screamed over me, and I felt the air that rustled my clothing and mussed my hair. I could even smell the grease on the wheel sets. I also felt the knot on my forehead from hitting the concrete as my bad arm buckled under me, unable to support my weight.

I remained on the pavement, examining a crack in the concrete and wondering if I made it when I landed. I was reminded of a Sylvester and Tweety Bird cartoon where Tweety patters up to the prone cat after he's fallen out of a building and says, "You in big twouble, Puddy Tat. You bwoke the sidewalk."

I considered calling it quits and letting someone else take over from here, but I've never been a quitter, even when common sense told me that was my only option. I pushed myself up — just to my knees — and crawled toward the door. I reached it in relative safety and stood to open it, then peeked out. They were still in sight, and Whelan was struggling to haul Mrs. Potter up the concrete steps to the midway, where they could disappear into the crowd. She wasn't making it easy for him, however, and I snuck up to the bottom of the stairs unseen.

Then I saw my opportunity. The handrail was unpainted stainless steel. I ducked back around the corner to take a deep breath, then peeked up at them and drew the stun gun. If she moved away from him for a second and he put his hand on the rail . . . But I was too far away. These little babies didn't put out enough amps to go through that much steel.

Mrs. Potter glanced back in her struggle and saw me, and I held up the device. Her eyes grew wide, and she shouted and grabbed the rail. Instinctively Whelan put his hands on hers to pry her off.

What was she doing? I ran up the stairs and was within six feet of them when Whelan saw me and cried out. Mrs. Potter flashed a look at me I'd never seen from her before, but there was no mistaking what she was telling me. No, I couldn't do it now, not while she was still gripping the rail! But she had other ideas and forced the issue.

"Now, Gil! Do it now!"

Whelan glared at her, and in a split second I read his eyes and knew Mrs. Potter was in grave danger. There was no longer time to think. I held the stun gun's electrodes on the rail, mouthing a prayer for conductivity, and pressed the trigger.

Blue lightning leaped from the electrodes and onto the steel handrail, and there was a shout from Dave as both of them crumpled to the steps. I released the button almost as soon as I pressed it and took the remaining stairs three at a time. Ignoring Whelan, I attended Mrs. Potter, hoping and praying that I hadn't stopped her heart.

While all my attention was on Mrs. Potter, Whelan came around and began pushing himself backwards up the steps, out of my range. I looked at him but let him go, and he stood on shaky legs at the top of the steps and stared at me for a second, his eyes betraying fear and confusion, then dragged himself into the crowd and was gone.

I checked Mrs. Potter's vital signs while I prayed out loud, encouraging her to be okay and asking the Lord to help her, and was relieved to find she had a pulse. A nice, strong pulse actually. *Thank You, Lord.*

In a moment her eyelids fluttered open, and she smiled wanly up at me.

"A real 'E' ticket ride, Gil."

The commotion generated by our actions had drawn a crowd, which in turn attracted the attention of two uniformed security officers. They ran up to help, and one of them radioed for the park EMTs.

"Go get him, Gil," Mrs. Potter told me. "I'm all right."

"He's too far ahead of me," I said. "The cops will catch him."

"No, it has to be you. They might hurt him. Please, he won't go far."

My face told her I didn't understand.

"He'll go to his office."

"How do you know that?"

"Are you questioning me, young man?"

"Absolutely," I said. "I need to know how come you're so positive. It's the cop in me."

She smiled and opened her clenched right hand. "I borrowed these from his pocket during the fracas." She was holding a set of car keys.

"You're a real klepto, Elizabeth."

"That's Dragon Lady to you," she said.

I patted her hand. "See you later, Dragon Lady." I got up and mounted the stairs, borrowing a radio from one of the guards, then took a deep breath and pushed through the crowd into the midway.

His office was dark and locked. I inserted my master key as quietly as I could, but total silence was impossible. Just try it sometime in a dark house at night. My only hope was that the sounds of the amusement park would drown it out.

I turned the knob, pushed the door open, and listened.

I heard nothing but the park noise behind me. Finding the light switch, I flipped it up, flooding the outer office with an off-white neon glow. The door to Dave's office was shut, and I moved toward it apprehensively, wondering what awaited me on the other side.

This door was thankfully unlocked. I decided to call out first and stepped off to the side, in the unlikely event he had a gun.

"Dave, this is Gil. It's over. Come on out now."

I waited for a response — a shout of defiance, the cocking of a pistol hammer — but there was nothing. I tried again, with the same answer. Dead silence.

Either he wasn't there, or he'd done something drastic. I had no choice. I shoved the door open and jumped into the room.

It was empty. Not just of Dave, but of furniture as well.

"You idiot!" I scolded myself. I should have remembered that he'd been promoted. He'd moved into his new office — Michelle's old one.

I hurried out and ran through the park to the Bijou Theater, irritated because I'd wasted time. By now he could have gotten his spare set of keys, if he had one, or fled on foot, or armed himself — any number of things. I made it to the outer door, which was open. The lights were on inside, but I didn't see Whelan. I walked in slowly, keeping an eye out in all directions, prepared for the ambush.

But I needn't have worried. Dave's door was open, and he was inside, sitting on the carpet in a ball, whimpering like a mistreated schoolkid. His hands were visible, and there was nothing in them.

No, there was something there. I hesitated. He held a knife, one of those Rambo jobs. It was poised, and the way he held it told me who he meant it for.

I sat in a chair near him, keeping both feet on the floor, and leaned forward slowly.

"Come on, Dave. It's all over."

He shook his head.

"You can't sit here forever. The cops are on their way. Let's drop the knife and walk outside with some dignity. What do you say?"

"I've ruined everything," he mumbled quietly. "I'm sorry, Gil. I don't know what got into me."

"Oh, I think you do, Dave. Greed and power got into you, and it was more than you could handle. But it's a done deal, Dave. You can't undo it. You can only stand up like a man and face the music."

He shook his head, and I saw his chest fill as his eyes closed. I'd seen that action before and recognized it as a suicidal man's last breath, the one he uses to draw in final determination. Just as his intake of air reached its maximum and his rib cage was fully enlarged, I shot out my arm and caught his wrist as he drove the knife toward himself. My hand locked on, and I squeezed.

He relaxed his hand, the knife fell, and he began to cry.

"What's going to happen to me?" he blubbered.

"Well," I said slowly as I kicked the knife away and let go of his wrist, "you're going to be arrested and go to the police station, then probably be charged with kidnapping, false imprisonment, assault with a deadly weapon — maybe some other charges, I don't know."

He spasmed and sniffed. "I'll go to prison for life! Why didn't you let me end it?"

"I don't know, Dave. Stopping you just seemed like the thing to do. And I doubt you'll do life. Nobody does life anymore. Besides, all your victims like you — Mrs. Potter and me. We'll have to see what happens. You don't have any prior convictions, do you?"

He shook his head. "Never even gotten more than a speeding ticket."

I grinned. "Yeah, I know about that. I gave it to you."

"Huh?" He lifted his tear-stained face to look at me.

"Yeah," I said. "But you accepted it well. You don't remember?"

"Now I do. I never made the connection. I've gotten a few of them."

"Well, anyway, your background will be considered. I daresay you've lost your job here. But you're still young, Dave. When you're, shall we say, a free man, you'll find another job. Look, Dave, I'll be blunt with you. Your problem comes from in here." I pointed to my chest, right over the heart. "You've got a sin problem. Some people manifest it with greed, some with drugs, others with rebellion against authority. But it's all the same thing. You need to get right with God."

"I told you, don't talk to me about God!" he spat. "Look at what I'm facing, and you talk to me about God? He doesn't care."

"Well, you have no one to blame but yourself for the predicament you're in. And as for God caring — I can't help but tell you that He does. He's not going to stoop down and touch you on the tip of the head and pronounce you innocent of these crimes. He can, however, deal with you *within* the circumstances you're in, even if they're of your own doing. He can change your future, Dave. He can change your heart."

"What good'll that do me now?"

"None, if that's your motivation. You need a changed life, Dave, something only

God can give you. It won't get you exonerated from the just deserts of your deeds. But it'll change you from the inside and make the rest of your life something you — and the rest of us — can live with."

"I don't know . . ."

"Of course not. I don't expect you to make a decision, especially not under these circumstances. Furthest thing from my mind. I'm just giving you something to think about, letting you know you're not finished. But you need more information. What God offers is in response to a commitment you make to turn from your past life, from your sin, to follow Christ. You can't do that if you don't know what you're committing to or why."

"What are you suggesting, Gil? That I become a namby-pamby Christian like you?"

I chuckled. "I'd hardly call me namby-pamby, Dave. Think about it. And I'm not encouraging anyone to be like me. I think you should worry about what God wants you to be. Remember, you have someone who loves you, whom you promised to marry. What about her? You were sincere with her, weren't you? Because if you weren't . . ."

He moaned. "Lois!" He dropped his head back into his hands. "She won't ever have anything to do with me again!"

I was relieved at his response. I was concerned that he'd just been using her, and I was inclined to box his ears if that had been the case.

"Can't say as I blame her, Dave, but I think you underestimate her. Maybe she'll give you a chance. It's true, you're not worthy, but . . ."

"It'll be different," he said.

"We'll see. Maybe when you're behind bars you'll feel differently. All I ask is that you give what I've said some thought. Ask the jailer for a Bible, read the Gospel of John. Or get ahold of me, and we'll talk. Only if you want to, of course."

He looked up at me with a question in his eyes. "I don't understand, Gil. Why didn't you beat me to a pulp? After what I did to you —"

I held up a hand. "That's the influence of God in my life, Dave. If it were left up to me, I would've at least knocked you a good one. Forget it, man. I hear the cavalry coming. Wipe your face and let's go. Let's walk out of here like men, okay?"

He nodded slowly, pressing his fingers across his cheeks. It was a pathetic sight, seeing him reduced to this. But it was encouraging too. There's hope for people when they're broken like Dave was. Harrowed ground, ready to plant. It's the ones with chips on their shoulders who are difficult, if not impossible, to reach. Hard soil where the seeds don't take root.

I helped him up, and we walked out together as a group of cops, followed by several park security officers, ran up the midway toward us, the nearby park guests pointing and jabbering, delighted to be getting more than their money's worth.

EIGHTEEN

I walked with Harry Clark back toward the security office, waving off a ride offered by the janitorial supervisor, Dan Harris, on his electric cart.

"What about Sally and Jerry?" I asked the security manager.

"They're both waiting in Jerry's office. We have a patrolman there with them. As soon as we get back, I'll send for them. Do you think Jerry's involved?"

"He says he isn't. But Dave said Jerry tried to sell out the park to the Hiromotos. Probably to Eric Hiromoto. The grandfather seemed like a pretty square shooter."

"Pretty serious stuff."

"Is it? Sounds like business as usual in the corporate world to me. But, hey, if it gets Jerry a one-way ticket to the bread line, I'm all for it. Is Sally okay?"

"She's fine, Gil. Jerry sat there like you told him to, complaining the whole time but not moving off his broken chair." Harry snickered, for the first time displaying something other than total dedication to the president of the park. Apparently he felt comfortable that Jerry wasn't going to be a factor for long. He recovered and continued, "I understand he was a little flustered when he found out she didn't have the stun gun. And he was really hot about the chair. Don't worry, the park will replace it, considering the circumstances."

"I wasn't worried, Harry," I assured him. Apparently I was unconsciously nursing my shoulder, and Harry picked up on it.

"Hurt yourself?"

"Yeah, some."

"How'd that happen? Dave do that to you?"

"No, he didn't. A door did this to me, so I retaliated with Jerry's chair."

"Oooh," Harry said in that tone people use when they've just realized what a dope you were.

We fell silent briefly, and I thought about what all this would mean to the park, what it would mean to everyone. Especially me. Not that I expected a promotion or anything, but surely the park owed me *something*.

That was a selfish idea, and I berated myself for it. After all, the whole thing was God's doing. He worked through me, gave me a brain that could figure things out and the physical ability to take action, and put me in the right place at the right time. If anyone owed someone something, I owed God.

As we approached the main gate, through which we'd pass before reaching the security office, we noticed a commotion outside. People were shouting and running. And judging by their direction of travel, the problem was at one of the ticket booths.

"What's going on?" I asked rhetorically.

Harry had seen it too. "Don't know. We better go see what's —"

Suddenly a white male wearing bicycle clothing darted away from the far side of the booth, his left hand grasping a large wad of cash, his right holding a small caliber automatic.

"The ticket booth robber!" I shouted.

"You're right," Harry agreed. He looked around, frantic. "Do we have any guards up here?"

"Probably not," I guessed. "They're all inside with the cops."

The robber sprinted toward some bushes, where his bicycle was probably hidden. Since there was too much ground between us, and he was obviously younger and in much better condition than me, there was no way I could catch up to him, and I didn't even want to, to be honest. My left arm still hurt pretty bad and would be of no use to me. The best I could hope to do would be to act as a witness and see where he went.

I told Harry as much.

"Okay, Gil. I'll get some help and see about the cashier."

I took off, ignoring my fatigue, but I hadn't even gotten to the gate when I saw the robber drag his bike out of the bushes and jump on it, start to ride off, then suddenly brake and wheel around to come back.

Then a city P.D. black-and-white skidded into view. The robber jumped off the bike, letting it fall, and ran directly at me, two cops exiting the car and pursuing him on foot.

Oh boy, I thought. *This is going to be good.*

As he ran, I could see money spilling from the pocket in his jacket as he reached inside, apparently to extract his gun.

You know, this was a great place to work!

He headed for the turnstile. What better place to lose yourself than in an amusement park full of 5,000 people? I pulled up to wait for him to come to me, trying to act nonchalant so I didn't tip him off. I could hardly wait. *Come to papa, you little —*

Uh oh. A uniformed guard was running up from my left. He'd heard Harry put the call out and was charging the main gate with his baton in his hand. But since he couldn't see around the corner, he didn't know that he and the crook were on a collision course, nor that he'd brought a stick to a gunfight.

I shouted to warn him, but he was so focused and the park noise was so loud, he didn't hear me. As precise as a drill team, the crook leapt the turnstile and darted around the corner just as the guard came from the other way.

I winced as they slammed into each other and went down. The crook's gun dislodged from his hand and flew to the painted asphalt, several important pieces breaking off — cheap Saturday night special that it was. The guard's baton slid a few feet away. The crunch was sickening, and I expected both men to just lie there, but to my surprise the robber — the smaller of the two — jumped up nimbly, apparently none the worse for the wear.

He groped for his gun as I began to close the gap between us, tossing it back down when he realized it was useless. I was ten feet from him when he spotted the baton and went for it. I did the same, but he was closer. Okay, he was quicker. I pulled up sharply and took a couple steps back when he held it over him like a club.

"Lousy technique," I told him.

"Back off," he warned, wagging the stick and ignoring my critique of his style. Over his shoulder I could see the cops hesitate at the gate. Behind me someone shouted, "Gil, catch!"

I turned my head in time to see D'Artagnon draw his sword. With his hand on the hilt, he tossed it toward me underhanded, point up.

It flew toward me, the hilt end remaining down because of its weight, and I caught it perfectly (and luckily) around the grip, in the same motion whipping it around and assuming the classic fencing stance I'd learned in college, though a trifle more casual than the instructor required in those days, just so I didn't look too dopey.

My opponent skidded to a stop, taking stock of me and his chances. He hefted the baton, slapping his free hand with it menacingly and trying to psych me out with a mean look. Yawn.

I pointed the sword toward his chest, flicking my wrist ever so slightly just to get the colored lights to dance off the blade, impressing the growing crowd that was forming a ring around us, many of them no doubt unaware this wasn't another stunt show.

Suddenly I was Jose Ferrer in *Cyrano de Bergerac*, one of my favorite all-time movies, as I formulated my strategy and became a little overconfident.

"Just to make things interesting," I told

the robber, "I'll invent a poem as we duel and end each refrain with 'thrust home.' And upon reaching the end of the final refrain, I shall thrust home even as I recite the words, and you will be dispatched once and for all."

"Don't press it, Gil," D'Artagnon warned from the sidelines. I waved him off. Actually, I was hoping to make the bad guy think he'd bitten off more than he could chew so he'd give up. I wouldn't have been able to think up a poem if I'd had a month.

I held my hand up to my opponent and stood erect, and he actually waited for me, so baffled by my actions that he forgot what he was doing. Seemingly disregarding him (while actually keeping a sharp eye on him), I rested the blade near my nose as I pretended to work out my rhyme, flopping my free hand around as if measuring my intended meter, then suddenly locked on my adversary's eyes with my own. I thrust my blade up in salute.

"Shall we then?"

He growled in reply and swung the baton, trying to knock the sword from my hand. But I relaxed and let the sword go with his swing, taking the force out of his blow and continuing it full circle, bringing it up behind his weapon and giving it a light tap, yet hard enough to maintain the momentum and send the baton further than he intended.

"Let's see now, how shall we begin?" I said thoughtfully.

But he didn't give me a chance, lunging at me immediately though he hadn't fully recovered his center of gravity. I sidestepped lightly and parried, and he stutter-stepped and turned, swinging on me again. Forget the poetry. My shoulder was hurting, and it was time to take care of this jerk. He wasn't getting the hint.

I retreated as he advanced, defending his every blow with flicks and twists of my wrist. He finally pulled up after all those futile attempts had winded him. He breathed hard and regrouped, and I could see he was becoming frustrated. It was about time to turn the momentum against him, to become aggressor instead of defender and bring this to a close.

"Had enough?" I mocked. He growled and raised the stick over his head as I suspected he would, and even as he began his upward motion, I pounced with a loud, distracting shout, stepping directly into him. The surprise was effective, for he hesitated, fearing I was about to pierce him with the blade, which he didn't know wasn't sharp. It was enough though, and I slapped the inside of his wrist on bare skin with the flat of the blade, giving it a terrific sting. The nerves and tendons being so close to the skin, he relaxed his grip involuntarily, and it was an easy matter to quickly swing the sword around in a backhand circle and do the same to the back of his hand. The baton clattered to the pavement.

He tried to regroup and dive toward me, arms outstretched like a linebacker, but I backpedaled and sidestepped to my left, and he overshot me. I immediately brought the knob on the hilt of the sword down on his head, then spun behind him and shoved him with my foot on his derriere. He sprawled onto the asphalt, and in a couple blinks cops and security officers were fighting for a piece of him.

With the crowd applauding the show, I held the sword in front of my face in salute and bowed, then tossed it back to D'Artagnon, who caught it and sheathed it with a flourish. Without comment I disappeared into the crowd and headed for the security office, making Harry run to catch up.

If I would never catch another crook, that was the crowning achievement of my career.

NINETEEN

An hour later Sally took me to the hospital, where I was just another patient waiting interminably to be seen by an underpaid but enthusiastic E.R. physician. Fortunately, nothing was broken or really messed up; it was just bruised like all get out. When that ordeal was completed and I'd been given all the appropriate shots and pills and slings and instructions, she took me home and left me there. She'd wanted to let me stay at her place, just to make sure I'd be okay, but I wasn't ready for that temptation, nor did I need a nurse.

Just to pamper me, Sally picked me up the next morning. I could drive, but Sally didn't want me to, so I granted her that concession. Harry had given me some time off to let my arm get better, but Sally said someone wanted to see me. I assumed she meant Mrs. Potter and figured Sally would be taking me back to the hospital, where the old gal was resting. She wasn't really injured either, but due to her age they had decided to keep her for a day or two.

But on the way Sally said, "Before we go where you've been summoned, we're going to stop by and see Elizabeth."

Ah, so there was somewhere else to go. I wondered where it could be, but Sally wouldn't give me any clues.

"I was told to have you there at 10," she explained. "We have an hour, just enough time to see how she's doing."

"She's chewing up nurses and spitting them out, that's how she's doing."

"Be nice, Gil."

"Don't worry, I will. She scares me. She has this really big ruler in her desk —"

Sally shot me a playful warning look, and I shut up. She pulled her Toyota into the hospital parking lot, and we walked in and took the elevator up to the fifth floor. Mrs. Potter was sitting up in bed, reading.

"Sally!" she said. "And Gilbert. How are you two kids doing?"

"We're fine, Elizabeth. How are you?"

"Fit as a fiddle and breathing fire!" She laughed, so we did too.

"So tell me, Gil, how did you figure it all out?"

I smiled wanly. "To be honest, Mrs. Potter —"

"My friends call me Liz."

"To be honest, Liz, I haven't. I figured out you were down there, and Dave tipped his own hand that he was largely responsible, but I still don't know why you were being held. I'm guessing it must be because you knew something, and Dave found out you knew and were going to tell me. But I don't know what it was you knew, and I don't understand what Jerry's involvement in it was, if any."

"Oh, you do know he's involved. You just don't know how deep," she said. "Come on, you mean your cop instinct didn't tell you there's something fishy about Jerry Opperman?"

"Oh, I suppose it did . . ."

"Darn tootin'! Jerry was trying to sell us out to Eric Hiromoto. He was poised to monkey with the deal, give Eric inside information that would be advantageous to their position, make the deal sweeter for the Hiromotos, including a controlling interest in the park. *Our* park!"

"How could he do that?"

"By turning over his shares of stock in the park. Add that to the amount we were going to sell Eric and his grandfather, and suddenly, when Grandpa's gone, Eric Hiromoto owns 52 percent of the park. In exchange Jerry was going to become chairman of the board in Japan."

"What about Dave?"

"Greed got to him. He got wind of something going on when Mr. Hiromoto was here and the roller coaster was sabotaged. It didn't take long for him to start adding things up. Then he came in to confront Jerry, but not for the park's sake. He wanted something in return for his silence. It didn't matter that you stopped Eric in his tracks. Jerry was afraid the owners would discover his attempt at treachery. Of course, with the old man out of the way, Eric might still have succeeded.

"Unfortunately, the morning Dave confronted Jerry, I came to work early. I happened to walk in when they were arguing, and Dave saw me and apparently thought I heard too much. I played dumb and was in the copy room when Jerry left, and I thought Dave had left too. Jerry didn't know I'd come in, but apparently Dave did. Right after I left the message for you to stop in and see me, Dave came out of Jerry's office in a panic. Ever since that roller coaster fiasco with you and the Japanese, he and Jerry had armed themselves. Dave grabbed Jerry's little shocker gizmo from Jerry's shelf —"

"Stun gun," I said.

"Right. He just whipped it out and *zap!*. That's all I remember for a while. When I woke up I was in the bunker apartment, so

I figure he must've taken me down there, not knowing what else to do with me. Dave fed me, kept me comfortable, but he was getting antsy. I don't know what he intended to do with me, but you forced his hand. It was touch and go there for a while. I have to admit, there were times when I thought he was going to kill me."

"So Jerry didn't know about you."

"I suppose not. No way to know for sure, though." She laughed. "Dave was a fool! If he'd waited, God would've taken me home sooner or later anyway. Probably sooner."

"What do you mean?" Sally asked, her eyebrows straining to meet in the middle.

"I have cancer, honey," Mrs. Potter said matter-of-factly. "Six months is all they give me."

Sally began to cry. "Oh, no, Elizabeth —"

"Oh, stop the waterworks, dear. God's been good to me. I don't have any complaints." She patted Sally's hand as Sally reached out to her.

It appeared Mrs. Potter was dealing with it fine, so I brought the conversation back. "Yes," I said slowly, "but their plot still would have been exposed. Dave couldn't let you go."

"Gil, let me tell you something — the owners of this place have done a real injustice to the memory of Mr. Golden. They don't know how to run this place, you know that. Why, Mr. Golden must be spinning in his grave. It would serve them right if someone wrested control away from them."

"You'd've let them get away with it?"

She glanced out the window, then sighed.

"No. I was going to tell the board. Monday, in fact."

"But you called me in," I said. "Weren't you going to snitch on them to me?"

"You? Whatever for? What could *you* do? You're just a security guard. Shoot no, Gil, I was going to tell you to have fun on your vacation and ask you to bring me home some trout. I love fresh fish."

We had a laugh about that, bittersweet as it was, knowing Mrs. Potter was dying. But she wouldn't let us be sad.

"Now you two go on. I'll be fine, and I'll be at work tomorrow bright and early. Shoo!"

She chased us out.

Sally was silent as we drove, unwilling to discuss Mrs. Potter except to say it was sad, and she also wouldn't tell me where we were going. But it quickly became clear as we neared the park.

"Do we have to?" I asked. "Just once I'd like to not go there."

"It's just for a few minutes," she said quietly. She was in no mood for a discussion, so I let it drop.

Parking behind security so I wouldn't have to walk all the way from the employee lot ("My arm is injured," I protested, "not my leg"), she guided me into the squad room, where Harry and Theo were waiting with two guys in suits and short haircuts.

"Theo, good buddy. What's up?"

"Gil, these guys are Feds. They want to talk to you about the plane crash."

"I already did that."

"We're not investigators, Mr. Beckman," said one of them by way of greeting. He was fortyish, Caucasian, and wearing a gray suit and a modest striped tie. Come to think of it, that described them both. "We didn't want to keep you in the dark regarding that plane crash, considering your efforts in saving the lives of those two foreign visitors."

"Are you sure you guys are Feds?" I asked. "Since when are you concerned about not keeping people in the dark?"

He cracked a slight smile, his allotment for the day, no doubt, but it faded quickly.

"A little humor. That's a good one. We're not the Feds you're thinking of, Mr. Beckman. We're with the State Department."

"Maybe you can explain something to

me," I said. "Why is it called the State Department when it doesn't have anything to do with a state? I've always wondered that."

"Ignore him," Theo said. "He thinks he's funny."

"Actually, he is," said the other Fed. I groaned inwardly. It's the kiss of death when someone from the State Department thinks you're funny.

The first guy continued, "We just wanted to let you know how much Mr. Hiromoto and his grandniece appreciate your work. I imagine they'll be sending you a personal message, but we thought you'd like to know that people high in the Japanese government are aware of what happened, as well as people high in this government."

"How high?" I asked.

"As high as you can get."

"Oh, the First Lady knows, does she?"

The Fed smiled again. Apparently he had one on credit he hadn't used the day before.

The second man picked up the narrative. "The F.B.I. has confirmed it was an act of sabotage. Apparently Mr. Hiromoto's son was going to great lengths to rid himself of his grandfather, for entirely monetary motives."

"Hadn't he been shipped back to Japan?" I asked.

"Yes," Theo said, "but he still had people here doing his bidding."

"Great!"

"We're in touch with the Japanese authorities," said the first Fed. "We'll be working something out."

I leaned over to Sally. "Sounds like a rubout."

"The details aren't your concern," said the second Fed.

"Don't want to know either," I said. "That's one secret you can keep."

They stepped forward and shook my hand in turn. As they moved to leave, the first Fed turned back to face me. "Keep an eye on your mailbox," he said with a wink.

"Why? Will I be letter bombed? Or am I a finalist in the Publisher's Clearing House giveaway?"

The Fed laughed again, completely devastating my opinion of Feds, and shut the door.

"Wow, a letter from the President," Theo said.

"I'd prefer a cabinet post," I quipped.

Harry Clark cleared his throat. "I hate to interrupt you two, but we have another appointment — upstairs."

He meant it literally and figuratively. Upstairs as in "with the owners" and upstairs as in up the stairs to the boardroom.

"What could this mean?" I asked Sally.

"I don't know," she said. "They're probably going to thank you."

Undying gratitude. That and eighty cents would get me coffee anywhere in town. Oh well, it might be fun. I stood up, and we all followed Harry out the door.

No one spoke as we trekked up the stairs to the boardroom, where the owners met once a week to listen to Jerry Opperman wow them with his brilliance. To my surprise, Joey Duncan joined us along the way. The walnut double doors were opened by an unseen force, and we followed Harry inside, Theo bringing up the rear. The owners sat around a large, highly polished walnut oval table, all of them looking in our direction. Jerry Opperman was conspicuous by his absence.

The chairman of the board stood.

"Thank you for coming, all of you," he said. "We know how busy you all are, so we'll get right to the point. Joey Duncan, please step forward."

Joey started when his name was spoken and took two small, slow steps toward them. "Yes, sir?"

"You were instrumental in the saving of Mr. Hiromoto and his grandniece. As they are business associates of this park, we owe you a debt of gratitude."

I leaned over to Joey and whispered in his ear, "Hold out for money."

He ignored me, and the chairman went on, "Allow us to present you with this plaque, commemorating your actions, and a small token of our esteem." He presented a plaque and an envelope, which Joey accepted somewhat tentatively. He was bewildered but pleased and thanked them as the board offered a round of applause.

"Sally Foster," said the chairman when they'd stopped. Sally was startled, since she wasn't expecting anything.

He went through the same speech, only it was tailored toward her efforts to rescue Mrs. Potter, and they gave Sally a similar plaque and envelope. I urged her to open it, but she told me to shush.

"And finally, Gilbert Beckman." I groaned, hoping they hadn't engraved *Gilbert* on the plaque. It was one thing to be saddled with that name, but to have it engraved on a plaque commemorating my heroism?

But no plaque was brought forth.

"Mr. Beckman, we want you to know what's gone on here since yesterday, to a large degree because of your efforts. Jerry Opperman has resigned as president. He apparently had been sidestepping the board during the negotiations with Hiromoto and was involved to some degree with Eric Hiromoto in the plots against his grandfather. That's a matter for the police to settle, and since Mr. Hiromoto was not involved in the deceit, the business deal will go through as planned. As far as we're concerned, however, we now have an opening at the top."

My head was swimming. They were about to offer me the position of president of the park, with my own parking space and heated vibramassage chair. This was more than I could ever have hoped for. My humble acceptance speech began forming in my mind.

"We have come to terms with the deceptions Jerry Opperman offered and have deemed it appropriate to extend an invitation to Michelle Yokoyama to return to us, this time as president. She has kindly accepted."

Rats. So close and yet so far.

"Because of the actions of Dave Whelan, he has also consented to resign, so we also are faced with another opening, that of senior vice president."

Okay, here it goes. Senior vice president, eh? I revised my acceptance speech a little.

"Raul Torres from the bank will be promoted into that position, which leaves a director's position available."

Well, I told myself, director of finance isn't so bad. Directors make good money.

"Harry Clark has graciously accepted a lateral assignment to that position, beginning next week. Which brings us to you. We have been remiss in recent years, placing unqualified people in positions when the truly qualified were assigned to tasks outside their expertise. You have shown yourself to be qualified, so we are offering you the position of security manager."

I was a little taken aback. In just under two minutes I'd been demoted from president all the way down to security manager.

"Well, I appreciate the offer," I said. "Can I have some time to think about it?"

"Certainly," the chairman said. "Take a couple of days. We understand you are recuperating. When you're ready to come back to work, we hope it will be as manager. Thank you. Thank you all." He sat down, and we were dismissed.

What? I thought. *No plaque? No envelope?*

We filed out and began returning to security, no one saying anything. When Joey couldn't wait any longer, he opened his envelope on the way.

"Check this out!" he exclaimed. "Four free passes — to Disneyland!"

I howled, then held a pretend microphone in his face.

"Joey Duncan, you've just scaled Mt. Everest with one arm tied behind your back and saved an entire airliner full of people. What are you going to do now?"

"I'm going to Disneyland!"

We laughed at our joke, but Harry grabbed the envelope from Joey.

"Let me see those." He looked at the tickets. "That's not Disneyland, you idiots. It's Disney *World,* in Florida. With plane tickets, car rental, and two weeks in the hotel of your choice."

"Whoa!" I said. "Quick, Sally, open yours!"

She did and got the same thing.

"Yippee!" she shouted, then said, "I mean, praise the Lord!" Then she calmly put her finger to her chin and said, "Now, who should I take?"

Everyone laughed, and we continued back to security and reassembled in the squad room, happily discussing our good fortune. Theo called me aside and took me into the vacant sergeant's office.

"I thought you'd like to know — Whelan 'fessed up."

"I thought he might. He's the type that likes to purge when he's caught."

"Want to hear about it?"

"Just the parts I don't know. How did he know Sally and I were going to the park when we left?"

"He wanted you to. He was setting Jerry up. He knew you'd figure it out sooner or later, so he thought he'd help you out a little with a bum steer. Before you and Sally had pulled away from Dave's curb, he had Jerry on the horn, asking him something that Dave knew Jerry would have to go to his office to get the answer for. He hoped you'd see him, figure out enough to think Jerry was responsible, and arrest him. That's why he lied about Jerry eating a lot of food."

"That part worked. But why did he help us figure out the stuff about the stun gun?"

"You caught him by surprise a little. He hadn't known anyone was outside to hear it when he zapped Mrs. Potter, but after he thought about it, he remembered that he'd left it in Jerry's office, where he found it. So by pointing you in the right direction, there was a chance you'd find that too. In reality, he didn't want to hurt Mrs. Potter. He just wanted to keep her hidden away until it was too late and the takeover was done."

"Then why'd he come to the park and show his hand?"

"He forgot one important thing — Mrs.

Potter would talk. He had to get her out of there before you found her."

"Almost worked too."

"Almost only counts in horseshoes and hand grenades." The only thing I could do was nod.

"So, what do you think you're going to do about the job? Are you considering taking it?"

"I don't know. I need to chew on it for a few days at least."

"Before you decide, I have a message for you from the department."

"Fitzgerald is so grateful to me for saving his life, he's decided he wants me to come back to work there."

"Gil, Fitzgerald doesn't know you saved his life. We're going to wait until his heart's strong enough to take the shock before we tell him. Besides, he doesn't care if you solve the Black Dahlia, prove who Jack the Ripper was, and get a confession from the gunman on the grassy knoll — he doesn't want you back."

"Then what's the message?"

"It's from the chief. He wanted me to tell you Fitzgerald's being retired. Chief says he'll be happy to entertain your application for reemployment."

"Detective?" I asked.

"You know better than that," Theo said. "But I don't think it'll be too long before I get you back where you belong."

"I'll give it a lot of thought, Theo."

"How can you pass it up? It's what you've been hoping for."

"I don't know. So much has happened these past couple years. A lot of things have changed. I believe I ought to really think it through this time, know what I mean?"

"Yeah, I guess. I don't blame you."

Sally came in. "Excuse me, guys. Gil, this just came for you." She held out a special delivery letter from the hospital where Hiromoto and his granddaughter had been taken. I opened it with raised eyebrows and read out loud, "Dear Beckman-san: Many thanks to you for saving my grandniece and me. We are forever in your debt and will never be able to repay your acts. A token payment would be insulting."

I looked up at Theo and Sally. "No, it wouldn't," I said, then resumed reading the letter. "But I can offer you something that will last forever, or as long as you wish it to last. You would be a welcome addition to my company. We deal with Americans on many levels, and we are prepared to offer you a job with our security department as liaison."

I looked up again. "I wonder what that entails," I queried rhetorically, then continued reading.

"That would entail the investigation and prevention of industrial espionage and providing security for our top executives as they travel to, from, and within your great country. You would be compensated amply for your services."

"I'll bet that's an understatement," Theo said. Sally was wide-eyed and silent.

"It would include," I read, "the car of your choice and unlimited use of company transportation."

"Helicopters and planes," Theo said.

"They have a yacht," Sally added.

I read on. "Your salary would be negotiable, and I believe you might enjoy your travels here and in Japan. You would choose where you want to live in each country, and we will provide the residence of your choice, within reason, of course."

"Of course," Theo echoed.

"I hope you will consider this offer. I again thank you, and remain, Sincerely yours, Kumi Hiromoto."

"That's amazing," Sally said.

"Incredible," said Theo.

"Wait, there's a P.S.," I said. "P.S. Should you decide not to join us, please allow me

the courtesy to have you and your compan-
ion as our guest at my home in Japan, as
soon as I have recovered sufficiently to return there."

I looked at Theo. "Boy, we'll have fun."

"Hey!" Sally complained.

I smiled and wrapped my arms around
her. "What would people say, us gallivanting
off to Florida and Japan together? Even if
we were good, no one would believe it."

She rested her head on my chest. "I'm
content just to stay here with you, Gil."

"This is touching," Theo said. "So, which
job are you going to take, Gil? As I recall,
you have an offer from Sheriff Thomas too."

"Can you believe it?" I said. "One day zip.
Next day four unbelievable job offers. Who'd
of thunk it?"

"God's at work, Gil," Theo said.

I looked at him. "Yes," I said slowly, "He
is."

"So, which is it going to be?"

"I don't know. I don't think it'd be fair
to choose without getting an opinion from
the person who's going to share the rest of
my life. Would you mind closing the door
behind you, Theo old buddy?" He smiled
wryly and complied.

I swung my head slowly around to smile
at Sally, who was staring at me, incredulous.

I sat her down in the sergeant's chair and dropped to one knee. "It's been a long time since I've done this, Sally, and then I only did it once, so bear with me if I mess it up."

Her eyes were wide, expectant.

"I love you, Sally Foster. And I think it'd be real swell if you'd consent to marry me. What do you say? Will ya, huh?"

You didn't actually expect me, Gil Beckman, to play it completely straight, now, did you?

Sally's smile was bittersweet, and she said, "Nah, I don't think so."

She took the wind right out of my sails, flattened me like a jackrabbit on the highway of life. My head began to spin. Then her smile widened.

"I love you, too, Gil. Of course I'll marry you." We both jumped up and embraced and tried to outkiss each other as a round of applause broke out in the hallway. I'd forgotten the sergeant's door had a large window in it.

"What do you say, Sally?" I asked when we paused for a breath. "Shall we honeymoon in Florida or Japan?"

The employees of Thorndike Press hope you have enjoyed this Large Print book. All our Large Print titles are designed for easy reading, and all our books are made to last. Other Thorndike Press Large Print books are available at your library, through selected bookstores, or directly from us.

For information about titles, please call:

(800) 257-5157
To share your comments, please write:

Publisher
Thorndike Press
P.O. Box 159
Thorndike, Maine 04986